I DIE BY THIS COUNTRY

CARAF Books

•

Caribbean and African Literature
Translated from French

I Die by This Country

FAWZIA ZOUARI

Translated by Skyler Artes

University of Virginia Press
Charlottesville and London

Note on the translation: All footnotes are those of the author.

Originally published in French by Éditions Ramsay as *Ce pays dont je meurs*

University of Virginia Press

Printed in the United States of America on acid-free paper

First published 2018

ISBN 978-0-8139-4022-9 (cloth)
ISBN 978-0-8139-4023-6 (paper)
ISBN 978-0-8139-4024-3 (ebook)

9 8 7 6 5 4 3 2 1

Library of Congress Cataloging-in-Publication Data is available for this title.

To my companion in exile

This story is inspired by actual events. In this account, the characters' names and circumstances are purely imaginary.

CONTENTS

I DIE BY THIS COUNTRY

I knew who they were. The clinking metallic sounds of their footsteps. I spotted the shifting movements of the guns bulging in the back pockets of their uniforms. Their mechanical movements. Their brows hemmed with suspicion. The police were bent over you—my father always lowered his gaze in front of them even though he had done nothing wrong.

Our neighbors were down below: Rose and Pierrot and his son, Gérard. I think I saw Mr. Zana. They watched the emergency crew and police bring us out on stretchers. They didn't ask questions. A little later on they gathered in front of the building manager's office. Quite shocked by our fate. Then they went away and closed their shuttered doors behind them.

The onlookers left as well, hardly convinced by the speculations Pierrot and his son offered. What could bring the lives of two young women—twenty-six and thirty-three years old—to an end? An overdose, probably.

The ambulance took off for the nearest hospital, the sirens straining through the streets of Paris. No one watched it go by. The retirees calmly went back to taking their dogs out to piss. The children didn't believe the ambulance lights shining through their windows were real—they thought the only real ones were on their television screens.

It's better to ignore the ambulance, whose loathsome work it is to announce that a future had just been shattered. That it's vain to try to protect oneself from death through savings plans, health insurance, exercise, cell phones, and sleeping pills.

The police returned to our apartment late that night. They rifled through our drawers. Examined the empty shelves in our rooms, opened the kitchen cupboards where we stored useless utensils. The unplugged refrigerator that was full of mold. They discovered the cat lying on a wheelchair and petted it attentively, as though it could give a statement.

They found all the details. All the same, nothing could clue them in.

They want to know. But know what? Why are they meddling in our affairs? These are people who never try to understand us. Do they really think we'll give them the key to our lives just as easily as we would the key to our drawers?

They didn't get an answer—they didn't look for very long anyway—and they left.

I knew they were going to come. Ever since the building manager's visit and our refusal to open the door for him. Though it could have been our next-door neighbor Rose. Rose is fascinated by the state's agents—she may have given in to her desire to call them.

At daybreak, I started telling you the story of our life in order to kill time. It was hard at first. Then the words flowed from my mouth, a depthless spring. And softly, slowly, I spoke to you. Just as one sings a lullaby. The one your mother hadn't sung since the day she left her village. Not because she had forgotten, but because it had lost its place in her life. Because, in vain, she tried to stifle her memories with deferred plans to return, fits of crazy laughter, and repeated trips through the department store Tati.

"Little sister," I began, "listen. Listen to the happiness drifting away."

We were under the illusion that we were happy. Only childhood keeps the notion of evil away, innocently casts the spell, and makes us believe that misfortune will never ever strike.

Amira, do you remember the glimmers of morning light that shone through the shutters in this apartment that used to suddenly wake to the sound of Mama's bracelets? Have you noticed how happiness can be at once simple and inaccessible? It was in the jingling of our mother's seven bracelets—in the light that danced around as she pushed back her sleeves or adjusted the scarf around her head so her hair wouldn't pick up the smell of her long-simmered *margua.**

We lived with the shutters open, the radio near the kitchen window constantly on, the smells of coriander and dried mint wafting out into the hall.

We filled the rooms with the commotion of our games of chase, of our quarrels in front of the television set, and then of our dreams on the same pillow. That is until our father's raised voice followed by Mama's cascading laughter—which sometimes came for no reason—brought Mr. Pierrot, our neighbor down below, to pound on the ceiling. Then our parents would fall silent. Sometimes Papa whispered things in Arabic—you only understood about half of what he said.

You were six, and I was thirteen. But we played together like twins. Despite your white skin and mine which was so brown, no one would have doubted we were sisters. An invisible wand set our movements and games to the same rhythm. A deep resemblance joined us, drawing its truth not from similar features—which didn't exist—but perhaps from the portent of a shared fate.

We climbed the stairs ten times a day, because in this Pari-

* A tomato-based ragout.

sian building that was like thousands of others, the elevator often forgot to work. Mama had a hard time keeping up with us. She wore shoes that were too tight and whose heels displayed cheap labels she forgot to remove. She repeatedly stumbled under the weight of her plastic bags. As she picked herself up, she cursed us. The warnings she gave us cut her breath and got caught in her throat.

It was probably because she begrudged this effort that Mama rarely went out. In any case, we preferred seeing her on the doorstep, welcoming us and wearing the *gandoura* she only wore inside, her honey-colored eyes circled with *khôl,* her henna designs refreshed. Everything she didn't dare show outside, Mama worked hard to show off at home. She spent hours in the bathroom, as though she were trying to rid herself from a filth whose source she couldn't identify. Amira, fascinated by Mama's beautiful shoulders, spent a long time scrubbing her back as women do in the *hammam.* When Mama left the bathroom, I would get her a Coca-Cola in place of one of the drinks from her country, and I would carefully place it on a tray that was brought back from over there just as the sheepskin was.

Then our mother would stretch out as if she were a princess from *One Thousand and One Nights.* We dried her hair, perfumed it with clove-infused olive oil, and plucked the white hairs that grew near her temples. Mama would look at herself in the mirror, rub Nivea lotion into her delicate, amber-colored skin, and then order us to leave so she could put on her underwear. We never knew how old she was, nor did we ever see her undressed. She said a grown woman should never be naked in front of a young girl or a teenager. We asked why, and she replied, "One cannot look at *it* without going blind." We never understood Mama's beliefs, but we knew we had to obey them just as one obeys all mysteries, because mysteries are of divine origin and quite simply from a maternal source.

Mama ran our house through the rhythm of her quiet demands, her long sighs followed by mysterious laughter, and her gold bracelets clinking together. The last ones she wore before she died. The ones we sold a year ago to pay for her burial. We never should have let them go. It was the last joyful noise Providence granted us.

Confined to the apartment, our mother gained weight, her fattened figure advertising the land of plenty's influence. Pierrot, our neighbor down below, sometimes pushed her cart to the supermarket, muttering, "Hey, Mrs. Djamila, these years in France sure have stuffed you. It's time for you to go home!"

"You're the one who should go home!" she would respond without thinking.

Taken aback, Pierrot would declare, "But I am home!"

"Me, too," she would reply without really understanding the meaning of her retort.

Once she got home, Mama would denigrate herself for how she looked. In Alouane, women envied her curves—she who had suffered from having so few as a young girl. Then she would get up, start folding her laundry, count her dishes, and sort through our notebooks as though she were getting ready to go back home. These imaginary departures soothed her. Afterward, she'd forget Pierrot's thoughtless remarks and the absurdity of her replies. She'd sit in front of her stove and watch steam rise from the couscous pot as she listened to the Egyptian singer Farid al-Atrache extol the beauty of the Arab countries he visited on his flying carpet.

With or without the extra weight, Mama always had trouble climbing the five flights of stairs in our building. For a woman whose grandmothers had forever lived in one-story homes, one hundred steps separated our century from her ancestral ways. One hundred steps that gave her migraines and made her head spin.

During the first few years in this apartment, she compulsively closed windows that were left open, fearing that an evil spirit would shove her out into the void. She railed against the *djinn*—her invisible cousins from back home. She chased them off with slammed windows, incantations, and fragmented Koranic verses that spilled from my father's prayers and that her memory collected, as she was unable to read and learn them on her own.

Mama tried hard in this new life. She really did want to set foot into our world, but she didn't want to give up tattooing that foot with henna.

I guess one reason she had Amira not two years after our arrival in France was in part so she could forget her people. Through this child she conceived of an activity that would make her forget she was in exile and distract her from the sight of Paris's gray roofs, which she could see over the promontory of her belly which grew with each passing day.

And so my sister was born not out of our parents' shared desire but instead out of our mother's secret machinations to brace herself against the surging memories of her native land.

Amira was tiny and fidgety. She cried all night as though she was refusing to be brought into the world just to heal her mother of the past. It wasn't until Amira started school that she calmed down. As soon as she was away from our mother, she seemed less nervous—more sure of herself.

Mama, a dreamer, would watch her vanish in the mornings, too tiny in her pink apron, her eyes hidden behind stiff bangs. In the evenings, our mother waited for us. When we were asleep, she would anxiously rifle through our pockets and sometimes discover that Amira had forgotten to eat the bit of the cake Mama had lovingly slipped into her pocket that morning. She would vow to scold her the next day, because she didn't understand how someone that age could have such a small appetite that they'd refuse sweets.

A few months after Mama arrived in France, my father told her she had to get rid of her veil. My mother's eyes went red with anger.

"Never—not ever! I will never strip myself bare!"

"But no one is asking you to strip yourself bare. You just need to take off your scarf."

"It's the same thing."

"And I'm telling you ignorance is a blight!" groaned my father before getting up from the table.

Mama couldn't bring herself to come around to her husband's line of thought. Walk around with her head exposed in front of men? There could be no greater insult to her family who remained back home. If her husband needed to see beautiful heads of hair, he could stare at the *roumia*s. But as far as she was concerned, she wouldn't yield. Her father, Cheikh Lazrag, said that a Muslim woman's hair was something apart. Woven out of a sacred material. Imbued with temptation. Blessed by Allah himself.

Papa redoubled his efforts. He ranted and raved, threatening to send her back to her village if she didn't take off her veil. Then he decided to go about it in a different way: he secretly asked Noura, his friend Béchir's wife, to do the convincing.

One afternoon, Noura surprised Mama at home. Wearing a flowing dress with a poppy print that accentuated her corpulence and adjusting her fake pearl necklace, the messenger solemnly took a seat on the family couch.

"I don't know why you continue to act as though you were still back there. The *roumi*s are not our people, and their gaze doesn't *work* the way Muslims' do. Do you want to know what my brother Mustapha thinks? He thinks the Christians' testimony, their religion, and their whole way of life don't matter in Allah's eyes. They are on Earth to look upon us before they pass into nothingness. So why should it bother you if they look at your hair?"

I don't know if Noura believed what she said, but she made a skillful attack. My mother nodded. In any case, she had learned that a woman shouldn't think too much, and she didn't try to oppose her husband or even wonder whether or not he was right.

Nonetheless, Papa was surprised to see Mama come through the door not only with her head uncovered, but also with a boy's haircut. The jet-black braids that had once fallen to her waist were gone.

"Are you insane! Who told you to cut your hair?"

"I thought if I had less hair, I'd have less of a need to cover it."

My father was speechless for a moment. As though he were seized by a sudden cramp. Then his face donned a mask of such pronounced sadness that he looked as if he'd just learned of a loved one's death. He left without saying a word. And came back in the middle of the night. Without warning, he grabbed his wife by the neck. He who had never beaten her now dared raise his hand against her. After her, it was my turn. The blows fell one after the next—more numerous than Mama's severed hairs.

The next day, our little family was called down to the local police station for disturbing the peace that night.

In the days that followed, Pierrot didn't approach my mother at the supermarket, nor did he push her grocery cart.

She put away her veils, and whenever she left the apartment, she exchanged her long *gandouras* for dresses that didn't reach her ankles—dresses that Latifa, a Moroccan woman introduced to her by Béchir's wife, made for her.

On the first day, she stared at herself in the mirror and asked me, "Do you think this is me? Are you sure this isn't someone else?"

I didn't answer. I didn't yet understand that she believed she was creating a double for herself through the magic of this new outfit. In a dress mere centimeters shorter than the traditional *gandoura,* she was no longer herself. Another veil—this one of strangeness—had been thrust upon her.

She watched herself walking down the street as though she were moving alongside a stranger. This was even more apparent in her hesitation—in her fleeting and curious glances at herself. With each step, she was likely calculating the distance she had strayed as she sought forgiveness from the omnipresent God, her ancestors, and her clanswomen. Did it occur to her to ask whether or not she—Djamila Bint Sidi Bou Ali, of noble parentage—should truly be compelled to wear this disguise? Nobody really knew. In any case, she never let anything show in front of Papa, and she never spoke with me about it again.

The only time she put her veil back on was when friends came to visit. Everyone who crossed the threshold into our apartment was expected to find themselves back in Algeria. And Mama believed she shouldn't attack men's modesty or ignite their desires, which were so quick to rise. These men from our religion claimed to have true vision and true desires. Guardians of the genuine key to sex and unadulterated orgasms. Great erectors before the Eternal. Their unrelenting stares made her skin bead with sweat. They had always possessed her, and they could even exert this right of ownership before her husband's very eyes. Perhaps deep down she believed her flesh did belong to them. So she had to put her veil back on, and she did.

On the other days, Amira and I were relieved when we saw her with her head uncovered, even if her clothes copied Noura's outdated look and bright red flowers.

We had just gotten out of school, where the principal lectured Louisa every day; she was guilty of having a veiled Mama by her side. "Where you live, they can go ahead and praise these *mashrabiya*s of reclusion! They can saddle them with meanings nobody understands, claim that they protect against desire, ward off the evil eye, compel God's esteem, and who knows what else. Pure imagination! Lies! And I should know. I lived in Algeria."

"I feel ashamed," Louisa said as soon as she was out in the courtyard. "I would give almost anything to see Mama disappear."

And in response to my indignant surprise: "I don't wish she was dead. Just gone—as if by magic—at the beginning of school. And then back again, just as mysteriously, once I get home."

I was just saying that my mother continued to feel foreign in this outfit. She couldn't get used to it. She often forgot to button the back of her dress. Her skirts were too tight around her waist and gave her gas. When her hair began to grow back, it blocked her gaze and got tangled in front of her eyes. She didn't dare brush it back, fearing this movement would be misunderstood as a desire to seduce.

Even though Mama had changed countries and clothing, her modesty remained as indelible as the tattoos on her hands.

She came from a maraboutic family, and tradition was a point of honor for them. In her village, which numbered no more than a few dozen homes, only the peasant women went out with their heads uncovered. She wasn't to do this, nor were any of the other female descendants of Sidi Bou Ali, whose name alone made the faithful throughout the plains of Souf tremble. Her marabout ancestor's renown was considerable, his list of blessings was long, and his place beside God was assured. His male descendants were called the Generous, because there wasn't a villager in need, a widow left without a bequest, or a beggar at the door they wouldn't help or whose burden they wouldn't ease. Every summer, brothers, uncles, and cousins distributed bags of wheat gathered during the harvest to the poor. And in the winter, the needy knew that within the marabout's walls, there would always be white bread and dates to calm their hunger.

Strangers to the family didn't know Grandmother Fattoum's face. During her long life, she rarely left home. And there was nothing to indicate that she was unhappy. Behind her walls, she held the same authority as her husband—sometimes even more—and she ran her household as a leader would. Men sought her advice on important matters—they sometimes asked her to make high-ranking people listen to reason. Grandmother would emerge from her doorway and set off to convince the stubborn one. She sat behind a curtain, disguised her voice with a handkerchief pressed against her mouth, and demanded she not be interrupted—that way no dialogue could be initiated. On the other side of the curtain, the man would listen in silence, sometimes nodding his head. He was instructed to give his final answer with a yes or a no. Very often, the former prevailed.

Lalla Fattoum's rare outings thus signaled that a serious dispute threatened the village, and everyone knew that it fell to this small fully veiled woman who proudly walked behind her husband to put an end to it.

No outsiders visiting Alouane could have imagined that the village's equilibrium depended upon a woman's actions. They judged only what they could see: when they passed by Fattoum's home, they didn't hear her footsteps or her voice. She became mute and handicapped and only communicated with soft handclaps. I can testify to this. When I was a little girl, I helped her by answering the door for her and asking the name of the person who was knocking or by going with Grandfather to find out.

Cheikh Lazrag received visitors in a large rectangular room whose walls were covered with tapestries recalling the pilgrimage to Mecca. Small watercolors portrayed the Prophet astride his winged horse, Buraq, flying through the clouds. Others evoked the ebony-muscled knight Antar ben-Chaddad's duels. The floor was covered with kilims, pillows, and cushions that had been scattered around the mats. Grandfather would sit in the middle of the tribal leaders and silently recite Allah's ninety-nine names with prayer beads. They seemed to mysteriously gleam, one after the next, with a beautiful phosphorescence as each name was spoken. Then Lazrag would get up. His guests would hurry forward to kiss his forehead and ask him to intervene on behalf of their ancestors so God would pardon their sins.

"And do they ever sin!" he confided to his wife at night. "With an abundance equal only to the degree of mercy they believe is owed them. They're in love with the misdeeds they ply in the shadows, yet they're boastful of the virtues they nail to their doors. They believe God will forgive them anything as long as the matter stays between themselves and Him. If a neighbor or outside witness gets involved, the gates of hell might close behind them. They tell me this, thinking I'm the only one allowed to share in their secrets without God taking offense."

Grandfather continued to talk, sensitive to his spouse's attentiveness but knowing all the same that she wouldn't bother him with her comments.

"So today I tried to frighten the grocer by telling him this story I heard from one of our shepherds. Listen to this, Fattoum; you will like it. Wanting to repent, a woman went to visit the angel Gabriel, and she told him that she had sinned a lot, so she wished for him to intercede before God on her behalf so as to assure her redemption. Without asking to know more about her sins, the angel agreed and went off to seek clemency for Eve's daughter. God listened and said, 'Go, Gabriel, and let this woman know that she will go to heaven.'

"Upon hearing the judgment, the woman was stunned. She asked Gabriel, 'Are you sure? Are you not mistaken? Considering my sins, God cannot so easily pardon me. Do you know what my offenses were?' And she recited the full list of the wrongdoings that marked her life. Among other sins, she confessed to having committed adultery and incest. 'Go back to the Lord and make certain of his judgment.' Gabriel relayed the conversation. The Only God fell silent for a moment and then declared, 'Tell this woman that her place is in hell.'

"Stunned, the angel ventured, 'But, Lord, I do not understand. First you had me tell Your creature that she would go to heaven. Today you will have me bear the opposite message. How can I explain this change?' And Allah said, 'Yesterday it was only she and I who knew the secret of her sins. She made the mistake of sharing them. Do you not know this, Gabriel? I only wrap my cloak of mercy around those who know how to wrap themselves in silence, and my pardon is dependent upon my creatures' discretion.'"

"Saviors of appearances—learned in concealed vice," Fattoum must have thought, but she never said so.

When Grandmother died, we accompanied Mama back to the village. She wasn't allowed to attend the burial. Only the men went to the cemetery. We had to stay at the house with her. The women gathered in the middle room and formed a circle around the body wrapped in a white sheet.

Amira couldn't stay still, and she wanted only one thing: to stir up trouble. Her fingers excitedly twisted her golden curls, and she entertained herself by making faces at everyone. Some of the visitors gave her stern looks. The peasant women were intrigued by her gray eyes and stared at them as though they were peering into the bottom of a magical well. Amira didn't resemble Djamila or Ahmed. "She's got the look of a bastard," one of the women whispered.

One might say Amira's unease fed upon these secret thoughts. Sensing the blend of annoyance and fascination she roused in these women, she derived even more pleasure in antagonizing them. She recited the poems she had just learned in first grade, and with her voice becoming steely, she pressed on with her repertoire of preschool nursery rhymes.

"Would you stop droning like a bumblebee?" shouted one of our aunts. "Are you forgetting that your grandmother is lying here?"

"She may be my grandmother, but I don't know her," Amira replied in broken Arabic. "I can't cry over some lady I've only seen three times in my whole life."

"Some lady! Are you listening to this crazy girl? God as my witness, I've never heard anything so ridiculous! To talk of one's grandmother with so much indifference—with such little care!"

"Care? I only care about people I know. I care more about our neighbor Rose than about Fattoum."

My aunt went red with anger.

"Did you hear that? She calls her grandmother by her first name! All that France has taught you is insolence and disrespect for your family. You filthy child! You bad seed!"

Amira didn't back down—she grew even more determined to provoke: "I don't have to love your family. Find me one passage from your religion that commands people to love their grandmother!"

A few women burst into dismayed laughter. Exasperated, my aunt gathered her skirt to stand, but then she stopped. She put her hand to her cheek and froze in a tragic silence. Her weakness drew from a lack of understanding. How could she describe my sister's attitude? There wasn't an appropriate adjective in her language. Crazy? Ingrate? Infidel? My aunt's vocabulary probably didn't include the word *free.*

Amira couldn't adjust to these strict rules of obligatory love and inherited feelings. She insisted that she didn't owe Fattoum anything because we lived too far away from her.

But I was born over there. I cried over Grandmother, and I know—especially now—that no one loses by loving, especially by loving the people in one's family. I think about the effect of Fattoum's rare words—they were like a secret balm on our existence. The force of her gaze protected us from evil—it could even have flooded Rose's merciless heart with love.

Mama was seated at the foot of Grandmother's body; she wore her traditional dress for the occasion. The village women came to offer their condolences, and they stared at Mama for a long time with dark suspicion and whispered to each other, "Fattoum never recovered from the shame her daughter brought when she married that old shepherd and went off with him to live in the land of the *roumis*."

"Leave, leave! As though that's what women are supposed to do with their lives. Our eternal home is here, where our ancestors are buried!" said an octogenarian in indignation.

"That's right," sighed her neighbor. "Ever since women got it into their heads to leave, God's wrath has been upon us. There are more fools are born in the village. And it rains less and less."

Mama caught every word, but it was easier to pretend she couldn't hear them. Perhaps she thought these women were right; it was true that she had been the first woman to leave her ancestors' land and venture outward. And where to? To the land of the foreigners—the land of the former colonists.

"How will you get by?" her sisters had asked her. "What language will you speak? How will you dress? How will you live without us and away from us?"

Fattoum didn't utter a single word. She simply studied her youngest daughter and sized up the unknown risks of the adventure that awaited. Her daughter only saw bliss and the very seed of happiness at the end of this road. "God, may she not suffer too much!"

When we went back for the funeral, Mama's dream had already shattered. But she never let on. Above all, she couldn't reveal that Fattoum had been right—she couldn't legitimize

Fattoum's concerns. She could never discuss her mistakes with her family—they boasted that no one in their family wanted to emigrate.

On the day of Grandmother's burial, the village women admired at length the seven bracelets Mama had forgotten to remove. In different circumstances, they would have asked her to bring some back for them. They greedily watched her sadness as if they desired it as much as they desired her jewelry. As if Mama's tears were as exotic as the strange things sold in French stores. Perhaps they looked at her with resentment. Maybe these people admired her at the same time that they condemned her for leaving. Even though they treated her as a renegade, they would have given anything to go off in her luggage.

Amira, do you remember visiting Grandmother's grave each time we went back? It was in the middle of the fields that surrounded the village—a peaceful cemetery that seemed happy to be so close to the living. The walls at the entrance had yellowed and given way in some places, and grass grew jubilantly between the graves.

Except for when a dignitary who was a native of Alouane died. Then the cemetery came to the regional authorities' attention and received a couple of hours of intense cleaning. Pickaxes swung between pathways, and whitewash brightened walls so as to welcome the prestigious deceased one.

Amira couldn't read the Fatiha* in Arabic, nor could she pray to God to grant her His mercy. One time, she shocked us by walking up to Grandmother's grave reciting "Our Mother, who art in Heaven," confounding our cousins, who thought they were hearing a French version of the Koran.

Some criticized her for having spoken the infidels' language in a sacred space. They told her this was the land of Allah, his Prophet, and his disciples. No people, no nation, no foreign language could be heard here.

I asked for forgiveness on behalf of my sister. She walked away, her cheeks saturated with the same guilty blush she had when she faced her little French friends' stares.

Apart from these moments when we were put in our place, we enjoyed the trips we took back to the village once every couple of years, most often during the celebration of Eid Esseghir after Ramadan.

Mama's village was peaceful back then—it seemed as if it

* The Koran's opening verse.

would always be that way. The two of us enjoyed cutting through the wheat fields, climbing the gentle hills, splashing in the streams, visiting the shrines, and yelling just to hear our voices echo. We didn't fear being reprimanded. Just like the elements, the adults were complicit in our joy and tolerant of our rowdiness. And that sky that seemed so severe with grown-ups became at once peaceful and clement for us, children that we were.

When my mother—who in France had picked up the obsession with keeping quiet even when there was no reason to—would motion to shush us, my maternal aunt would step in: "Let them be. You can't act like you do over there. Maybe you think I don't know what I'm talking about, but you're wrong. I heard from my friend Yvonne that kids in France don't have any freedom—everything is decided for them well in advance and they're controlled by parents, schoolteachers, monitors, educators, and God knows who else."

"It's so they're better prepared for the future," Mama answered.

"It makes them unstable! I heard from Yvonne that when kids are five years old, they have to start seeing weird doctors called 'spychiatrists.' They're forced to confess everything at such a young age that once they've grown up, they don't want to talk anymore."

Yvonne was a former colonist's daughter, and since her childhood my aunt had worshiped Yvonne. For a long time, Ms. Bonvilles served as such a moral and aesthetic model for Hadria Bint Sidi Bou Ali that everyone started calling her "Yvonne." When the real Yvonne left Algeria for her native region of Brittany, she continued to correspond with Yvonne the Algerian, who paid her nephews to read and translate the letters arriving from the town of Roscoff. My aunt had amassed so much information on the former "Motherland" via the *pied-noir*'s daughter that the few educated people in Alouane saw it fitting to call her father's house "the Archives of France."

As for us, we brimmed over with gratitude for Aunt Yvonne's wisdom, and our excitement grew. There was no longer any question of putting the brakes on our free rein. We ran around barefoot, we followed Sadek the Mad all the way to the edge of the village, we threw stones at the donkeys, and we traipsed through the wheat fields, unapologetically trampling them. Only one thing disgusted Amira and me: unlike our cousins who did it with unabashed pleasure, we couldn't bring ourselves to steal fruit from the orchards.

"It belongs to other people," my sister would say with all of the authority of her eight years. "We have to respect that."

Amira's scruples made our companions laugh.

"Tell me, aren't you called a little thief over there? And you have the nerve to tell us what to do here!" one of the girls replied.

Then they began insulting us in Arabic. They made fun of Amira's skin—white "like an onion"—and her "pig face." Some girls suddenly grimaced and yelled, denouncing our parents as cowards who deserted this country in order "to go and beg from the French."

Lacking skills in the art of the invective, we gave in without saying anything. We were unsettled by the violence of the comments. They were continually punctuated with the word *sex*, doled out in a dozen synonyms. The arguments quickly petered out; other games beckoned us.

On the days when our walks separated us from the adults, our cousins reveled in finding ways to shock us. To our horror, they'd get each other off in the fields: they'd lie on top of one another—groin against groin—and rub against each other for a long time. Each girl moved her hand between the thighs of the other or slid in a blade of grass. One day Slimane, the old sharecropper's young son, came along with us to chase the dogs from our path. Suddenly, little Myriam told him to kneel and play with her between her legs. It was an order, and he did it without a word, just as though she'd asked him to tie her shoelaces. She sat down, legs spread, and the boy moved his finger inside.

I remember our embarrassment—the stupid expression on our faces, Amira's and mine. My sister pretended to be lost in thought, watching a few wheat stalks. I turned my head toward the cemetery. We tried not to meet each other's eyes. Finally, my sister walked off with such slow steps you'd have thought her legs each weighed a ton. I followed her, my ear still catching Myriam's malicious laughter—in it rang a total indecent joy. This dissuaded me once and for all from believing the wisdom of grown-ups, for they held her to be an obedient and subdued child.

I know I never talked about sex in front of my sister. And if we grew up together knowing everything about our bodies, we never talked about such things. That expectation was silent but insistent. My mother made sure of it.

But today, what turmoil could these images rouse in our bodies, where desire no longer finds its way and hasn't for years? Our female cousins would be astonished by this confession. And our male cousins even more so. For them Europe is less a land of civilization and more a gigantic whorehouse. But they're wrong. Unlike the young women from over there, we grew up without knowing pleasure.

It wasn't until after Papa's death that adult desire was revealed to us. My mother's desire—no matter how well hidden—was buried within her. Yet she dreamed, my mother, often out loud, and we heard her call out to her husband and then moan. He had just abandoned her; she was still young. The first night, we rushed to her bedside in alarm. We timidly called to her. Her eyes closed, asleep, she pressed herself against her mattress, and her body twisted lasciviously. Sometimes she breathed heavily like the dog that belongs to the neighbors above us. Two lesbians who moved in right after Mama passed away, praise be to God! What would she have thought if every night she heard as we did the two women's cries of pleasure interrupted by a dog's strange barks. My mother would have died, not of frustration, but of shame. For how could she accept this "absolute vice" given that she felt herself to be the repository of centuries' worth of virtue? The whole time she lived in France she refused to believe things like this were real. She closed her conscience off from the impostures of sex, judging all of its public displays to be unspeakable and dishonorable. She avoided seedy streets, turned her head away from any poster where the tip of a breast stuck out, recoiled like a dragon's fiery tongue away from any red sex-shop sign, and she would aggrievedly distance herself from any bench where a couple was kissing.

"Really, don't they have a place to do that?" she grumbled.

"Sure, but they like doing it in front of other people," replied Amira.

Mama didn't give in to the provocation.

"It's like during Ramadan," she continued. "Would I ever think of eating in front of someone who was fasting? No. That would be to lead the person to temptation."

"All you have to do is not look at them!" Amira concluded, irritated.

"But it isn't me who's looking at them. They're the ones pretending I'm not looking at them."

Typical of her reasoning.

That said, she tried so hard to conceal her longing, but it surfaced anyway. When I was twenty, I understood better than Amira (who was still a teenager) that Mama's fainting spells had to do with her deprivation, and that her wild fits of laughter—more frequent than they were before my father's death—were nothing but her body's piercing cries. At the time, I said nothing, because she seized upon a pretext and insulted both of us in Arabic—this language of peasant women and sharecroppers' wives, women from whom she was not descended: "You sluts! Females without men, like houses without roofs."

Amira barely understood Mama's rough dialect, but she cynically ventured, "We'll find husbands. We just have to go out at night sometimes."

"At night? Like those debauched French girls? Never! What would your father say?"

"But he's dead!"

"He'll find out all the same."

So, according to my mother, this was male authority. It survived beyond the grave—death didn't diminish its power.

In truth, my father undoubtedly wouldn't have said anything. After spending twenty-five years in France, he saw a certain number of concessions as inevitable. He couldn't live in what was called a free country and hold his daughters prisoner—he couldn't conform to French customs and also impose his rule as an Arab patriarch. He understood that he had to turn a blind eye to the length of our skirts, to our escapades in the nearby Georges Brassens Park, and to our occasional trips to the movies if he didn't want to drive us off toward the hospital or out into the great wide open.

But Papa also had to play the role of the Arab father. Just to remind himself that he wasn't French. So he would raise his voice from time to time, he knew how to perfectly ignore us as any self-respecting male did, and he didn't hesitate to turn off the television at the slightest sign of a kiss on the cathodic screen.

Yet Papa didn't have much time to properly fulfill the role of father. He woke up at five in the morning, cleansed himself, recited his morning prayer, and left without a sound. As soon as he was out of the building, he pulled on his beret, blew air into his hands, and set off toward the Porte de Vanves metro station.

When he arrived in front of his factory, day had barely broken. He split off toward the only bistro open at that hour. Mr. Paul, the owner, knew his clients well. He went in, walked up to the counter, squeezed himself in alongside his Maghrebian brothers—even if there was more room farther away—ordered a coffee, and said thanks.

"At least with you," said the owner, whom Papa had disarmed with kindness, "we don't have to worry about hearing you yelling every morning. And even less so about serving you a glass of red. Now that, that is a true Muslim!"

"But a bad Frenchman!" Béchir, Papa's compatriot, cynically replied. "One day I was unloading in Saint-Germain, and I overheard a large gentleman with glasses telling the waiter, 'They cannot claim to love France without a glass of red and some Camembert in hand.' I, for one, share this point of view."

"Nonbelievers and bad philosophers like you . . . it ruins life for all of us!" the owner replied with satisfaction.

My father wasn't even listening to them. He had these moments when the very fact of being present at that instant, in this country, at the counter of that café, on the corner of that street, or in that metro car filled him with doubts. But he shooed them away with the back of his hand; stoned the devil, that purveyor of bad thoughts, with verses; and to assure himself that he truly was in a reality other than that of his ancestors, Papa pulled his Basque beret more firmly down over his head. Walking past glass doors and seeing the reflection of his tall silhouette with that hat on, he faced the fact that he really was on French soil.

He took only a half-hour break in the middle of the day. The rest of the time, he passed through kilometers of hallways to stock spare parts, label boxes, and load crates onto carts and trucks.

He returned at nightfall. He talked for a few minutes with the building manager, a Portuguese man, in exile just like him. Then he took off his beret and climbed the stairs. As soon as he was in the apartment, spent, he pulled a chair up to the table and had his dinner served to him.

However, we knew that Papa fulfilled his conjugal duty just as well as he fulfilled those duties required by his boss, because we heard the sound of our parents' bed quietly squeaking late at night. My mother seemed to give willingly of herself, which isn't to say she didn't enjoy it. Even though she never looked like a seductress at night, she often glowed in the morning.

When I was fifteen, I began to suspect that these moments of intimacy bolstered my father's self-confidence. Under his roof, in his bed, on top of his wife, he once again became the master of his destiny. He could give orders and be obeyed. Ask and be heard. Reprimand us without worrying about our reply. Belch and spit at will. Have his feet washed without being seen as acting macho. In short, he returned to his place in the hierarchy as soon as he hung his Basque beret behind the door.

Imprisoning his wife's body under his was also his way of regaining possession of his country. The country he would never forgive himself for leaving.

I was the only one to discern the green reflections of Alouane's prairies in my father's gaze. Maybe because he truly wanted me to read his eyes. In any case, I had a hard time imagining him expressing his nostalgia in front of Amira; she was too young and often indifferent with respect to him. Maybe the gray-green color of my sister's eyes didn't inspire his trust in her. He was even less likely to confide in Mama, because she would've hated him. His gazes spoke to me.

The accident had to happen. A fall from six meters as he was restocking supplies in a warehouse. Spine broken. Eight months in the hospital. Daily visits where Amira unwillingly accompanied Mama and me—she couldn't stand the smell of the antiseptics and hated the icy nakedness of the white walls. We'd stay for hours, looking at Papa as he stared back at us. My mother's eyes lingered on her husband's inert muscles, on his hair that had turned white even though he was only forty-five years old, and on his vacillating pupils. She broke her silence to sigh and repeat the same phrase over and over again: "Allah willed this." Her monotone voice told us next to nothing about how she felt.

They came to tell us that visiting hours were over and we needed to leave. Amira's face picked up some color. Mama stood up, ending her watch. She mechanically dusted off the sheets, and shoved under the bed the straw basket she had filled with prepared meals and honey cakes that Papa's diet and hospital regulations strictly forbade.

When we saw my father leave the hospital in the wheelchair, we understood the tragedy that had just struck us. The only thing left for us to do was to calculate the extreme fragility of our situation.

My father without work. No one could help us. We were in a country where we had no family, no important connections, and very few friends. Amira had just started middle school, and I was struggling through my junior year of high school even though I had already turned eighteen. Mama had given herself over to her role as wife and mother; it kept her completely occupied. Tradition and her old way of life back in the village also distanced her from the notion that a woman should be required to make a living.

We constituted a strange kind of harem, without a man. I heard this from our neighborhood grocer, a young bearded Moroccan who had traded in a university education at the Sorbonne for rows of fruits and vegetables: "A harem, in the economic sense of the term," he explained to me, "is a community of women who ask to be protected, fed, and taken care of."

Handicapped and housebound, my father no longer existed in the eyes of others. His presence diminished, and his shadow shrank day by day. He no longer dared to raise his voice at us or to boss us around. Unproductive, he quickly persuaded himself that his authority, just like the lower half of his body, no longer had any effect.

Constrained to this immobility, he often tilted his head toward me. At night, I did my homework on a corner of the kitchen table, not far from his wheelchair. I don't know what I reminded him of or what secret answer he sought in me, but I often caught him contemplating me. I didn't dare look at him for too long. A somber copper coloring took over his frozen face—it was like the memory of a prior sun turned to ash. My eyes couldn't rest upon his features without taking on the impression of his past, like the way closed eyelids fleetingly hold on to halos of light.

His nostrils would tremble at every burst of Mama's laughter. Then his features would once again become still, and the light in his pupils would go out, just like the eyes of the blind.

I spent every day I had off with him. Sometimes when he was next to the window, I'd hear him sigh as he looked up over the rooftops. I'd go sit at his feet with the cat. He would caress my hair, lean over me and whisper, "I will never have a view of Sidi Bou Ali's cupola from here. These Paris roofs are nothing compared with the plains of Souf. And I'll die without ever seeing them again."

During these long afternoons when he would stare unremittingly out at Paris through his window, I would travel with him through his past.

There once was a village surrounded by fields. Plains and valleys wrapped around it in a loving embrace. Hills and wooded slopes kept the desert at a distance.

For three-quarters of the year, green blanketed the village of Alouane, where the descendants of Sidi Bou Ali—may God's mercy be upon him—lived. There was a grocery that served as a general store, a small *hammam,* a pond where the boys waded during the summer, a Koranic school within the walls of the mausoleum, and a railroad track.

The earth provided good wheat that made the neighboring villages jealous. Wells had been dug every two hundred meters to water the orchards where, each season, the best-tasting fruits and vegetables grew: round and succulent peaches, apricots that children would sink their teeth into even if they were still tart, and tomatoes as firm as virgins' breasts. The people would pick olives while singing praises to Sidi Bou Ali. The peasant women placed the olives in their laps, the boys played soccer with watermelons, and the little girls took advantage of the harvest to look at their reflections in the well water.

When the harvest was good—and it often was—the wealthy families would slaughter sheep and give *sadaqa.**

They would send a messenger to nearby villages to announce the annual marabout festival. On that Friday, Cheikh Lazrag himself would go to the marketplace in the neighboring town of Séra and look at the cattle. He handpicked the finest steer, paid, and then left. Tradition dictated that the animal walk the fifteen kilometers on its own, bringing itself to the foot of the sainted man's tomb. The animal always made it, arriving at the walls of Sidi Bou Ali, and no one was ever able to explain the mysterious powers that spontaneously led it to its destination.

* Charity.

It took many men to slaughter it; the women made couscous for the whole village. In the afternoon, the important *fellah*s washed up, shaved their legs with a blue powder dissolved in water, and ran a bit of *khôl* below their eyelids. They put on their starched *djellaba*s, wrapped their heads with beautiful *chèche*s, and ushered the young males from their brood out in front of them; the men looked proud, their hands crossed behind their backs.

The wives removed their jewelry, covered themselves in white veils they pinned at their chests with brooches, covered the lower part of their faces with small embroidered veils, and followed their little girls' footsteps.

Everyone sat on kilims covered with sheepskins and cushions to watch the horseback riders from Séra perform acrobatic feats to the sound of the *baroud.*

On that blessed day, the poor delighted in semolina, which they rolled between their fingers and drizzled with honey before letting it all melt in their mouths. The children crowded around the makeshift stands that had been set up in front of the mausoleum. Buzzing like flies, they swarmed around burlap bags filled with dates, grilled chickpeas, sunflower seeds, and green- and fuchsia-colored stick candies that were so delectable and so sweet they left an indelible mark upon each childhood in Alouane.

It was during one of these *zarda*s given in honor of Sidi Bou Ali that Ahmed first saw Djamila's eyes. He had of course seen her when she was a young girl; he clearly recalled her round face surrounded by a black mane and her thin silhouette. But ever since she had turned thirteen, she no longer went out except on rare occasions like this one or on spring afternoons when she played in the surrounding hills accompanied by her sisters and cousins. The young girls entertained themselves by racing over the hills, their silk *safsari*s* wrapped around their shoulders. They coursed over the other side like a flight of doves, their white veils floating through the air as though ready to take

* White silk or linen veil.

flight. Ahmed hid behind a rock on the next hill with a bunch of boys his age and watched them.

This young man had inherited a plot of land. Granted, his two hectares were nothing compared to the estate of Lazrag, Djamila's father. Despite nearly a century of French dominion, no colonist had succeeded in appropriating Lazrag's land. All the same, the land Ahmed had inherited gave him the advantage of escaping the humiliating life of a sharecropper. When he was young, he went to Koranic school. But he attended the state school for only one year; his parents objected to seeing him cover the fifteen kilometers to the school in Séra and then back again on a donkey who threatened to die, an innocent victim of a type of knowledge no one saw as being useful.

Ahmed had, therefore, spent several quiet years tending his father's sheep in the meadows. He entertained himself by tracking game, listening to the echo of his songs, and playing small flutes he fashioned out of reeds. At nightfall, the sweet and nostalgic melodies reverberated from valley to valley and from hill to hill until it was time for the young shepherds to bring in their herds and close the corral gates. The dogs would finally fall silent, and the village would sleep peacefully.

He was the only son among seven daughters, and his aging parents would soon leave the land and the small farm to him; he would do his very best to run it. He was also fortunate to have a trim waist, strong and masculine shoulders, and healthy, bronzed skin. When he passed through the village, he could be sure that dozens of young girls were secretly watching wide-eyed through the keyholes of their doors as this twenty-year-old man passed by, proud as a peacock and built like a Berber warrior.

Sadly, this good fortune was not to last. Rain grew scarce, and the wells dried up. The war for freedom lit the fires of rebellion everywhere, and every young Algerian male could be counted among in the nationalist ranks. Determined to kick the French out of the country, the *fellagas* spread rumors about the colonists' imminent departure. Some hinted that as soon as the French were expelled, the land would become state property.

Ahmed was forced to sell his sheep one after the other, and his youngest sister secretly left for the capital in search of work. No one knew what became of her or what trade she plied. She never returned to Alouane.

It was during this time that a man known as the Stranger returned to the village. He was called this because of an exile that had lasted fifteen years. In the early forties, the real Yvonne had taken an orphan named Gharib away with her in her luggage. She made a real hustler out of him, and he came back speaking better French than the colonists and driving a huge car Cheikh Lazrag called "the tank." Djamila's father never went by that car without saying a contemptuous *Aoudhou billah.**

During Gharib's second visit, the village was bordering on famine, and the country seemed concerned only with thoughts of independence. The Stranger found his childhood friend to be in despair.

"Ahmed, come to France with me," Gharib suggested. "The *gouirras* need strong arms like yours, and you'll have no trouble finding work. You can't spend your life staring up at the sky—its rains are more capricious than a woman's moods."

Ahmed thought about his parents, his sisters, and Djamila,

* I put myself in God's hands.

whom he still quietly desired. His heart immediately began to bleed from the anguish of exile, and the sky over his village shone with that splendor it had right after a rainstorm.

But he couldn't shake his friend's proposal. He thought that his departure would protect his parents from want. Better yet, it would make the villagers forget about his former status as a shepherd. As soon as he came back with his fortune in hand, Cheikh Lazrag would no longer see any disadvantage in granting him his daughter's hand in marriage.

Ahmed returned five years later. His features were slightly worn, but he was as handsome as ever. His hair was smoothed back with Brilliantine, and a tie with a tiny Eiffel Tower print flapped over his chest.

He showed up in the roar of a brand-new Renault he parked in front of his parents' house. He attracted the same crowd of curious onlookers that once flocked to the old festivals of Sidi Bou Ali.

The next day, his mother knocked on the Lazrags' door.

Fattoum said no. And her daughter the opposite. "No, a thousand times no," said Fattoum. "Never Ahmed, son of One-Eyed Touirellil; he used to be a shepherd."

"Yes, him, only him, and no one else," replied Djamila, who had succumbed to the emigrant's charm.

Fattoum asked those around her to explain her daughter's persistence in wanting to marry a boy she didn't know. But Djamila remembered Ahmed's insistent gaze during the marabout's festivals, and also the glimpses of his proud figure she'd seen through the keyhole.

She was convinced that Providence had sent her this man so she might escape from strict maternal control and from an imprisonment that had lasted for years.

The young girl threatened to drink bleach if her family continued to deny her choice. Then she came up with a less wretched death and swore that if she couldn't marry Ahmed, she would throw herself into the well. His origins may have been modest, but he had traveled and made some money, and marrying him would allow her to straddle the sea and place one foot on the other side of the Mediterranean. Before her, this was something no woman in Alouane could have imagined doing.

Fattoum feared a scandal and yielded before the cortege of women who came to her door a second time with Ahmed's mother in front asking for Djamila's hand.

The Lazrag family made half-hearted wedding preparations and, within one week, got it all over with. Djamila was granted a single night of celebration rather than the customary seven, and the horseback riders from Séra whom had been called in for the occasion didn't fire off the *baroud d'honneur.*

After her wedding, Djamila quickly became disillusioned. Offering thousands of excuses, her husband refused to take her back with him. The year after I was born, he reiterated the same refusals. This lasted for six more years.

Mama complained about the distance that separated her from her husband. She decried the injustice of having her little girl grow up without a father, like an orphan. She said that she was wasting the best years of her life. And she was right. She saw her husband one month out of the year. And during this month, he was carried off by his family, who clung to his wallet, his sisters, who competed with each other to please him, and his friends, who looked to him to perpetually enliven their parties with stories of his exploits in the land of the *roumis*.

Nobody ever thought Ahmed might be lying. But still. He made things up. He embellished his stories with details that painted his life as one of leisure, money, comfort, and respect. You know, France. Only Lazrag listened stone-faced to his son-in-law, his fingers nervously passing over his prayer beads.

Ahmed would return at night exhausted from telling so many contrived stories. He'd whisper some gentle words to me and run his hand through my hair. It was calloused. It was probably the only thing that conflicted with his tales. The only sign of his time in France. But no one seemed to notice. Then he would go to his wife's bed.

My mother, who remained with her parents, lived a strange existence, in which happiness ran alongside frustration. Her moments of happiness amplified the pain of her future solitude. She mourned her husband's imminent departure ever more intensely as her body blossomed for thirty days beneath this man's gazes, his caresses, and his desire, which was renewed at the thought of leaving her.

"Take us with you," she begged. "How long are we going to live like this? I'm married to a ghost who appears once a year. All the neighbors who used to be jealous of me are making fun of me now. They at least can say that for every night and every morning that God makes, they have a man in their bed."

"Give me a little more time. So I can get things ready. I want to give you the welcome you deserve."

Mama felt hopeful once more and hid her concerns from her mother, who secretly delighted in keeping her under her roof. She spent her days dreaming—she would lie on a mattress with her body in Alouane and her spirit wandering the streets of France. The very thought of her future stay in France made her entire being quiver as though she had been brushed by a magical feather duster. She imagined setting up her future home with real beds and wooden chairs—items unknown in Alouane. She dreamed of placing a vanity in the middle of her bedroom and filling its drawers with powder puffs, jars of cream, and lipstick. And—an absolute must—she imagined hanging copper saucepans on the kitchen walls; she believed their gleam summed up the cozy comforts of home and of things falling into place. The calm flow of a perfect life. Copper saucepans had been her greatest wish ever since she'd heard that city people were just as proud of their collection of pots and pans as they were of their offspring. Mama devoted the rest of her peregrinations to finding me a good school and then walking with her head held high under the Paris sky. These dreams were as shimmery as Fattoum's fabrics. They immersed her soul in an ocean of phosphorescent bubbles.

Then the day came when Grandmother faced up to the fact that her daughter Djamila was going to leave. She began having convulsions, and they thought they might need to call a doctor to examine her for the first time in her life. She refused, threatening to kill herself if a man other than her husband touched the slightest bit of her skin.

By nightfall Fattoum had calmed down; she put on her veil and slipped outside. Intrigued by this unusual outing, I followed her. She set off toward Sidi Bou Ali's mausoleum. She went inside, lit a candle, and leaned over the sepulcher. Her tears dampened the green cloth that covered it.

I stayed behind the mausoleum's door. Grandmother probably knew this departure was the prelude to her daughter's suffering, and to ours. She didn't see any need to upend tradition. To open the door to adventure. She didn't want Djamila to condemn her descendants to the hardships of living abroad.

She got up, tied a knot in the green cloth, and whispered, "My God, may she leave in peace and return safe and sound. May she not stray from the right path, for she would tarnish the family's honor. Shame is so difficult to erase. It outlasts life. Sidi Bou Ali, my cherished one, hear my prayers. Protect my daughter."

She went back home without noticing my presence. I followed her as though magnetized by her premonition.

Mama at last discovered what her husband's life on French soil was really like. She learned that he was a simple warehouse worker in a car factory that had agreed to hire him based on Gharib's recommendation. Much later we learned through his friend Béchir that up until our arrival, our father had lived in Sonacotra employee housing, where immigrants were crammed four to a room without heat and sometimes without electricity.

Ahmed was lucky. When Béchir left Paris for a larger place outside the city, he left Ahmed his three-room apartment. In a low-income housing building right near the beltway on the south side of the capital. My father, who had hastily furnished it with the bare minimum, rubbed his hands together as he watched Mama walk in on the first day.

"You should be thrilled to be right in the middle of Paris. Your people normally live in the outlying neighborhoods, which aren't very safe. You're two meters from the metro and right above the supermarket. A veritable Ali Baba's Cave."

My mother was stunned. She bitterly thought that Ahmed had forgotten that back there, her family's home was in the very heart of the village and had rooms large enough for her brothers to play soccer in. And in Alouane she never even would have gone grocery shopping, because she didn't go out and because others took care of that for her.

However, she decided to tally up these changes in silence, and she told herself she had to forget her past if she wanted to begin her new life on the right foot. She erased from her mind the roads that led to her village, she refused to think about the calm evenings she once spent on the patio, and she wondered whether the walks along the hillsides and the festivals of Sidi Bou Ali had ever really happened at all. No, all of that meant nothing . . . A mirage. She should no longer think about it. It would be better to find a cure: a baby's smile, for example.

Mama got used to her three rooms with low ceilings that crawled with cockroaches. She no longer dreamed about the comfort of handwoven rugs from Alouane. In the absence of real armoires, she stacked suitcases, boxes, and plastic bags on the worn linoleum floor. She found only the bathroom to be to her liking, and she took refuge there whenever she could. Instead of trips to saints' tombs, she had to make do with jaunts though the Tati department stores.

The handsome and proud boy who was said to have become a "man" while he was abroad was nothing more than one Maghrebian worker amongst others, employed by a French boss who called them all by the same first name: Momo.

Ahmed had shrunk a bit. He didn't have the same imposing presence as before. He sat with his chest bent over his plate, as if he were nearsighted. Even the voice he once used outside the home had changed—it had become thin and feeble. His gestures lacked assurance, and when he expressed his frequent—and rarely justified—thanks to people, he avoided their eyes.

Yet at home, he made an increasing number of remarks and allusions that attested to his male power, meaning he let us know how wrong it would be to challenge his decisions. Though Djamila tried to conceal her thoughts, Ahmed knew what she was thinking. He reminded her that because he had the advantage of having spent more time in the *roumi*s' country, he knew better than she did how to appreciate the blessings of their situation. He was determined to convince her how good her situation was and how ungrateful she would appear if she rebelled.

"Don't speak your language in front of the French," he added, "they don't like that. Don't be like one of those wide-eyed cows from back home. Take better care of your home. I'm working myself to death to keep you all alive, so how about a little respect?"

"But it's normal that you work—you're the man . . ." Mama saw fit to respond.

"And what about our neighbor Rose? Is she a man? She still works."

"Well, I didn't think about her," my mother naïvely confessed before continuing, "but it's not the same thing . . . "

"Perhaps," interrupted my father, "but it's time for you to make some changes. For years you asked to come here—now you need to do what everyone else does. Stop being apathetic. Right now. And give thanks to God that you're in this country. You're not in your *bled* anymore."

When the word *bled* came from my father's mouth, it didn't just mean Alouane or the plains of Souf—it meant the whole of Algeria. It didn't evoke the provincial scenery's charm or relief, nor did it evoke the land's majesty. Hearing this, you'd think Al-Jazair was nothing more than a small place with worn-out customs. Though his country was four times larger than France, for him it represented only a deplorable emptiness, much like poor people's wallets. Did Ahmed really believe what he was saying?

In any case, over the course of months and years, this was how my father endlessly worked on transforming Djamila, a true descendant of Sidi Bou Ali, into a banal immigrant.

Mama didn't say a word to her family about her disillusionment. Women in her family learned early on to endure and to conceal. Especially when she had chosen her own fate. She had wanted this marriage—she would accept the consequences. Giving others the opportunity to badmouth it was out of the question.

So she hid her disappointment, forbade us from making the slightest mention of our real living conditions, and forced herself to forget Papa's unkind remarks.

Every time she went back to the village, her arms were loaded. In the months before her departure, she had but one concern: to shop. To race through the cheapest stores and make certain she didn't overlook something her cousins, aunts, or distant relatives might enjoy. Even Sadek the Mad got a box of tea or a bar of chocolate.

Mama bought tennis shoes and fake leather jackets for the horde of kids that rapidly proliferated—this caused her insoluble calculation problems—shiny scarves for the older aunts, T-shirts for the fans of American soap operas, stainless-steel silverware for the future brides, cloves for those suffering from rheumatism and toothaches, and zucchini seeds for snacking during Ramadan's long evenings.

She started with the Saint Pierre market, visiting the boutiques one by one, big and small. She followed the elevated metro line in Barbès, going all the way to Stalingrad Square, where Tunisian shopkeepers toiled in wholesale shops. She devoted Sundays to visiting the flea markets in Vanves and Montreuil.

As soon as she returned home with swollen legs but sparkling eyes, she unwrapped the purchases one by one, admiring them and deciding upon their recipients. Though Amira and I didn't raise any objections or ask if we could have anything for ourselves, she eagerly pointed out that she'd gotten great deals, but we weren't to whisper a word about that to our relatives over there. Then, she meticulously packed up what she'd bought and prayed to God to keep the evil eye away.

In the weeks before the trip, we camped out between suitcases and shopping carts that reached the ceiling; dishes and kitchen appliances that cluttered the hall; and bags of almonds, hazelnuts, and tea crammed into laundry baskets.

Mama didn't much care about improving her home; she barely thought about what might be missing from our life in Paris. She spent money in order to construct an image for herself over there. An image of a rich and happy woman. My father didn't say anything about this marketing operation. His pride and virility also depended upon it.

It was a big deal when my parents' car drove into the village after a difficult boat ride from Marseilles and eight hours of driving plus one extra hour on dirt roads. Even the new mayor (an old member of the FLN who had been offered a position in Alouane and a promotion to the mayor's seat by independent Algeria as compensation for fighting in the *maquis*) went out to the front steps of his official residence.

Every head, young and old, looked up. The state's farmers left the fields. The married women suddenly remembered that they were supposed to visit a cousin; they put on their veils and hurried outside. The day's only train blew its whistle three times and then once more. Children formed a procession, running behind my father's mechanical engine—a Renault sold at a 30 percent discount to employees—and yelling, "Vive la France!" It was the mid-seventies. But in Alouane, with the exception of the mayor and a few public figures, no one seemed to know for sure whether France had left or if it was still camped out in the country.

A crowd gathered in front of my grandparents' home. On

the patio, my mother—who instinctively went back to her old way of sitting cross-legged—waved her arms about as though she were working the stock market floor or an auction house.

"Six casserole dishes for your aunt. So she might intercede before God on my daughters' behalf. Here's what your big sister asked me to bring last time: hair rollers and a blow-dryer. These socks are for the youngest girls. This silk remnant cost me a lot of money—it's for your oldest daughter's trousseau."

We watched Mama's impressive distribution of these gifts that robbed us of our own personal comfort. Yet we sat there like enthroned queens. Lofty and generous, as though we'd been born to bring happiness to Alouane's people. Mama seemed so happy. So we were happy, too. As soon as she finished handing out the gifts, our mother lay down on a cushion covered with sheepskins and waited to be tended to by the women of more humble backgrounds who had come for this very occasion. They waxed her and applied her henna and her *harkous*, that black dye that lengthens and deeply darkens eyebrows—something she never would have allowed herself to have outside of her Parisian apartment.

Once she was dressed and made up in the style of Alouane's women, she didn't look like our Mama anymore. It was hard for us to tell the difference between her and our aunts, and we hesitated for several seconds before speaking to her. She answered in Arabic with a such a marked intonation and a cadence that was so quick and so saturated with the local accent that even my father didn't understand her. Her ancestral language's words rushed out. They bloomed on her lips and flitted about like butterflies, swirling around and then returning to her, as though her ear clung to what her mouth had said out of the sheer pleasure of hearing herself speak.

Then Mama left, barely interested in our needs. She deliberately refused to spoil us in front of women who were bestowed with one too many offspring and couldn't afford the luxury of excessive displays of affection.

After the distribution of gifts, no one was happy, of course. Mama had forgotten someone, showed a preference for someone, favored someone, or had simply made a mistake. The next day, she realized she had made more people in the village unhappy and jealous than happy and satisfied. One thing was certain: no one ever said thank you. As though they were owed all of this. Worse yet, it wasn't unusual for others to tell her the mean things certain members of her own sex were saying about her.

"Really. Who does she think she is? And how does she get all this stuff if it isn't with *haram* money?* After all, it is but God who gives, and we only accept God's blessings."

* Illicit.

The vacations in Alouane were our window into our parents' past. Once every two years. Mama thought that this was enough for us to feel like we were solely from Al-Jazair.

Once we got back to Paris and were outside of our building, we rid ourselves of our memories from over there, of Mama and her lingering smell of couscous and henna, of her bracelets' jingling, and of the singer Farid al-Atrache, whose voice haunted the kitchen.

In short, we were no longer under our parents' rule. We were immediately aware of this: at school the orders were slapped down in another language that followed a different set of logic. We also measured this by how hard it was for the teachers to pronounce our last name: "Touirellil"! They did try but later gave up. Some systematically called us "Bin." Just as people called my father "Momo."

I suffered more from this than Amira did. Because I'd lived over there when I was a child, and I would've given anything for my name to be pronounced correctly, just once.

My mother enrolled me in kindergarten one year after I came over from Algeria. I had already turned eight. I didn't know a word of French, and I had to start with the youngest class.

When the teacher introduced me to my future classmates, they raised their heads in unison. I saw as many questions in their eyes as there were black curls in my bushy hair. I didn't yet grasp that my candy-pink apron must have equally shocked them. As for my deep brown skin, it wasn't as surprising because there was a Senegalese girl who had come into the class before me. I rushed to find the first empty seat.

I was older and taller than the others, and my height became a source of torture. I looked for any reason I could to sit down, and I stayed perfectly still on the playground because I was convinced that even the smallest movement would bring a torrent of insults and jokes down upon my overly exposed head. I would have given anything to stop growing and to win my classmates' respect; it seemed to me that the cost of their increased respect would be that of my shrinking in size.

For years, the giant I thought myself to be was silent in class. During this time, I must have used up all the manna of silence God grants a life. I paid such extreme attention to what was going on around me that I always had the impression that I was like one of Alouane's cows watching the train going by in the distance.

I felt so different in terms of my language, my looks, and my thoughts that I only had one challenge over the years that followed: to be like everyone else. To not mar anything in this language, in this landscape, or under this French sky. Waiting for the miracle that would make me small, ordinary, and non-existent.

Amira was born on this land's soil, in one of its hospitals, under its haze, and with its language. But our parents came from somewhere else, and we desperately tried to explain to my sister that she wasn't like the French, but she was convinced otherwise. My sister with gray-green eyes and such straight hair.

To our classmates, we were first and foremost the "foreign sisters." Out of our last name with the strange consonance, they crafted a fatal verdict, a chemical bond that joined our fate. Little by little, we ended up not resembling those around us. Instead, we became bound together before the same stares.

Just like in a game of "spot-the-difference," our classmates struggled to identify what we contributed to or took away from the French landscape. When they finally tired of this game, they left us alone. Because we used the same seats, we eventually broke down some of the barriers. In class, we—Amira and I—became full-fledged "friends." It was only when we left school and met the adults who were holding onto the fencing that the differences were truly reestablished and the dividing lines were redrawn.

Mr. Eccars was enchanted by Amira. She was the most outspoken student in the middle school. She surprised the teacher with her intelligence, her sensible replies, and—sometimes—her insolence.

Mr. Eccars listened to my sister speak and nodded his head. He understood her before she even said a word, and he was moved by her gaze, which sometimes got lost in space. He encouraged her to study, assuring her that the future was hers. He pushed her—"like Balzac's heroes," he insisted—to "conquer Paris."

But very quickly there were complaints about segregation and discrimination. It was so strange! Mr. Eccars was accused of favoring Amira. The principal even suspected this pureblooded

Frenchman of being in league with the former "suitcase carriers" of the Algerian War. We later found out that Mr. Eccars was Buddhist and believed in reincarnation and was convinced he had been an Arab in a past life.

Even my father treated him as an infidel; he threatened to take his complaints of metaphysical harassment and attempts to convert his daughter to the Department of National Education. The teacher's response was that our father understood nothing about History and even less about the mysteries of Reincarnation.

"Furthermore," he bitterly concluded for our benefit, "if your father sees so little importance in the sympathy I feel for the Arab people, he must be a '*harki.*'"

My sister and I didn't understand. A few years after my father's death, we listened to the news about the demonstrations and strikes staged by the *harki*s' children. It wasn't until then that we got it. At that very moment, we also got that Papa's friend Béchir bore the same label. My father knew it, but he never broached the subject with him. Undoubtedly so as not to open a wound that prevented his compatriot from ever returning to Algeria. No. At home, we didn't talk about it. The old shepherd was loath to pass judgment. He let the people with diplomas and the professional accusers do their work—work he didn't approve of.

The other French teachers were not at all sensitive to the Arab cause. They had a special fervor for "the Republic." For a long time, I thought this was a real woman who—along with her twin sister, "Secularism"—was worshiped by the French. Their names constantly jumped off the pages in the intellectuals' newspapers, but I didn't understand their exact meaning until I was over thirty years old.

In any case, the teaching staff wanted the school's mold to be perfect and without any flaws. So that every student left school stamped with the same official seal. Once students grew into adults, they could get away with all sorts of deviations—it was no longer their institution's concern. Students were made to understand that later on the best among them could chase after originality and make a career out of dissidence under the incontrovertible mark of their "individuality."

We knew our case was different. With goodwill based either on principle or naïveté, the teachers strived to fashion us after the same model. To make us into children of the Republic. Sadly, as soon as we stepped outside of the school, everything rushed forward to nullify their laudable efforts. The mold shattered at the threshold of our apartment, where my father's prayers hummed. It fell apart when it came into contact with the blood-red henna that coated Mama's hands. It became more deformed each time we visited Fattoum's.

We were no longer at home in Mama's "school," where lessons were supposed to be diffused by magic. We were at this one, this boastful school of the Republic. We learned about everything there—except about the Arab world. We heard the most extraordinary stories—except for those about our parents' past and our country's history. Sure, there were stories about well-armed warriors, but they were different from the ones decorating Grandfather Lazrag's sitting room. There were Zola's and Flaubert's heroes; we could like them without pretending to identify with them. There was the beauty of important French sites and monuments that were worth praising, though all the while acknowledging that they didn't belong to us. We caught glimpses of the most amazing things, but not of our future as the children of immigrants. We could list France's technological feats and recite its great industrial progress and flourishing postwar economy without mentioning the massive immigration that assured this prosperity.

In short, what filled our little heads as we sat in our seats in the Republic's school seemed like those streams that tributaries accidently create. Those streams that flood fields and make flowers grow. Those streams couldn't convince anyone of their legitimacy, being as far as they are from the maternal source. Nothing in French history coincided with our own, and yet the whole of History was to be recognized in it. We were to describe the state of our soul in a language that wasn't interested in us. I couldn't find a way to resolve this distance, and I struggled in this strange space where I found neither a past nor any hope for the future.

Amira was different from me in this regard. For her, there could only be clear solutions. As these were scarce, a mysterious affliction threatened her.

Maybe it was because of her desire to provoke that my sister remained fragile and tiny, and that at the age of twelve, she first began to refuse to eat. Unless there was something else going on. The doctor didn't know how to explain it. Unable to identify the affected organ, they'd probably have to return to the source, on the mother's side, in order to find this rotten bit of soul.

Amira nonetheless struggled with her health during her second year of middle school. Some days she came home pale, joyless, and with no appetite. In vain, Mama would put full plates of food in front of her; she didn't remember the uneaten packages of cookies she used to find in her little girl's pockets when her daughter was much younger. No one asked Amira questions, and no one yet knew how to read the early signs of her illness.

That year, Amira wanted more than anything to convince her classmates that she was like them: a hundred percent French. It was no longer enough to claim that her small differences could be "enriching," as Mr. Eccars put it. She had to prove that she had no connection to her parents' origins.

She dared to do what I never would have. With an innocence that quickly won others' hearts, she fearlessly asked her teacher, "Don't you find that Arabs lack civilization?"

"What? But civilization began in your part of the world!" Mr. Eccars replied, outraged.

Unsatisfied, she decided to ask her mother the same question but in a different way, as if she were able to teach Amira about her identity.

"I'm going to ask her who we are."

"She doesn't even know who she is. How do you expect her to tell you who we are?" I replied.

"Who you are?" my mother responded, eyebrows furrowed. "What is it with these ridiculous questions? You're my daughter, of course! Pure-blooded Algerian! Descendant of Sidi Bou Ali, may God's mercy be upon him!"

And she laughed so hard that *khôl*-darkened tears rolled down her cheeks.

Beyond the realm of Sidi Bou Ali, Mama didn't know how to go any further back or how to explain to us this past that

Mr. Eccars claimed was glorious, as though this Arab people had nearly conquered the world. My mother never went to school, but she knew how to cook and how to laugh for no apparent reason, and above all, she also knew how to keep quiet. It was probably during her moments of silence that she taught us what we didn't know of her country. But this wasn't enough. How were we to have learned the village customs we were so unfamiliar with, acquired the ancestral knowledge we encountered but once every two years, or grasped the personal journeys my parents kept secret? By what kind of magic did the Touirellils expect us to carry on their traditions, their language, and their prayers without guiding us through their country's school of life?

Eventually, I wound up telling myself that if Allah had wanted to work a miracle, he would have taught us everything about Algeria in one go, and we wouldn't have needed to go back there or to transform our poor mother into Mr. Eccar's interpreter. After all, this was how the Prophet Mohammed received the Koran. Without ever having learned a thing. And he hadn't yet become an immigrant.

Determined to provoke, Amira shot back at Mama.

"I love Christ," she announced to irritate her.

My mother brandished a ladle and reminded Amira that it was blasphemous to speak a name other than that of our Prophet.

"He preaches love," continued my sister.

Indignation nailed Mama to her stove.

"He's the son of God!" Amira said in a rising crescendo.

My mother nearly fainted.

Our parents had a hard time with us. Amira lost all interest in studying, while I never had any. It wasn't that my head was in the clouds. I wasn't less intelligent than the others. But somehow I understood that if I didn't study too much, I wouldn't deepen the divide between my parents and me. I wouldn't add another exile onto their exile. Separation from their country and from their offspring. I refused to know, just as Amira often refused to feed herself. I wanted to become a nurse so I could take care of my parents when they got old.

So I was an average student, not standing out in any special way, trying hard not to reveal a distinguishing feature in the middle of a painting in which we were asked to appear good and without ambition.

Amira stopped talking with her teachers. She was no longer outspoken in class. She befriended girls with names like Anne and Aurélie. Gracious, thin, and lively, she easily drew people in. I found out that she had people call her Marie and that she invented an Italian origin for herself. Those friends who had never seen our parents had no reason to doubt her. She was like them: light skin, gray-green eyes, light brown hair that cascaded over her shoulders.

"May God protect your daughters," Béchir's wife said to Mama one day. "They're kind like you. They don't have bad friends, they don't run away, they don't get into trouble."

Mama didn't say a word about Amira's wavering grades at school or the problem with her appetite.

As though she were speaking to herself, Noura quietly added, "My children have forgotten the respect they should show their parents. It's as though living in this country makes them superior to us. I can let it go, but Béchir is unhappy. He isn't a father—he's a wreck. And the more he gives in to them, the more lost they become."

Mama listened to Béchir's wife with compassion and a touch of disdain. As far as she was concerned, and in spite of everything, she felt no shame in showing us off in Alouane's *douar.*

The middle school principal was the one who said something. One day when I was picking Amira up from school, he asked me to step into his office.

"Your sister used to be brilliant. She no longer talks in class. I've also been told she doesn't eat anything at lunch. Are there problems at home? Are your parents getting along?"

I didn't know what he was implying.

"Amira's grades are down, and she no longer seems able to put forth any effort in class. Her mind is elsewhere. I'm putting you in charge of informing your parents."

Papa had Amira come into the kitchen and sit across from his wheelchair. He gently said, "You don't know how lucky you are to have the opportunity to go to school. I only went to school for one year in Séra—I know the value of knowledge. So you are not going to quit . . . "

"You will not disappoint us," Mama interrupted, as she cut the wings from her chicken. "Think about your cousins who have managed to study. They'll have important jobs later on, and they'll look down on you if you drop out."

She added bitterly, "If only you had a stronger constitution . . . But with this puny body, the only good thing you can do is study."

She was probably thinking about her village, where a woman's worth was determined by the abundance of her curves. She had been fattened up by her family, who had made it their job to give her future husband an ample bottom and fleshy thighs. This was all in vain. In spite of their efforts, Djamila got married when her waist was still thin.

Papa didn't add a word.

It's true, we never should have clashed with the Republic or its auxiliaries. Regardless of my father's mediocre pension and the existential pick-me-ups Mama got in Alouane, we could have quietly continued on.

In the supermarket book aisle, our neighbor Pierrot found *Je veux rentrer à la maison* (I want to go back home), a book by some Christiane Collange, a journalist by trade. He gave it to us with the instructions to think it over with our parents. In his rush, he misread the title, telling us it was "Je veux rentrer au pays" ("I want to go back to my country").

In the book, the lady stated that she was tired of the working world and had come to prefer life at home. This was the year I forced myself, in spite of everything, to pass the *baccalauréat* exam and graduate so I could find a job—under no circumstances did I want to shrivel up at home. During this same season, my mother found herself frequently needing to go out to make sure the household errands were taken care of. In an attempt to comfort her over my father's accident, Noura took her out to visit the public gardens. Sometimes the two followed the Seine, venturing all the way to the Georges Pompidou Center, where they would boldly sit between the flute and *darbouka* players.

No one in our house understood that there were women who could find joy in willingly staying at home without there being the threat of a whip.

Or without fate's tragic intervention. The intervention that a few months earlier had brought our father home on a stretcher, his spine broken.

Troubles immediately came one after the next. Amira's refusal to eat became evident to all of us. It was beyond any doubt that my sister suffered from a mysterious affliction. Because her lack of appetite was sometimes accompanied by uncontrollable urges to eat. But as soon as she got ahold of herself, Amira ran to the bathroom and threw it all up.

My mother quietly began looking for a traditional healer. Papa sidestepped her. He had a doctor come over.

"Your daughter suffers from anorexia. It's a common disorder among young girls her age. But she might grow out of it."

He didn't say much more than that, and he left. The man of science may have given my sister's illness a name, but neither our parents nor I understood its meaning, causes, or implications.

That same week, irritated by Amira's look of disgust in front of a dish Mama had carefully prepared to spark my sister's appetite, my father asked, "How could it be that in a family of solid Algerians you are . . . what did the doctor call it?"

"Anorexic," I stated.

"Where we come from, this is an unknown illness. It only strikes people from here because they're without faith or heart."

Mama nodded in agreement. She also firmly believed that anorexia was an illness for romantics, atheists, and the suicidal. A French illness. I thought, "Not only does my sister want to live *like them,* she's making it so she can suffer from the same illnesses."

Amira started going through periods in which she seemed to have lost all joie de vivre. We had to go and get her from school several times because she had fainted. At home, as soon as Mama forced her to swallow anything, she shut herself in the bathroom and vomited the very little she had ingested.

Her repeated absences from school had the expected consequences. After being called in by the principal numerous times, being asked to put an end to her absences, and being unable to produce doctor's notes, she understood that she no longer had a place at that institution. She felt she'd been kicked out and didn't show up at the new middle school where she'd been assigned. At the end of the trimester, I was cramming for my *baccalauréat* exam. And so we all found ourselves back at home. Without having chosen to.

My father's accident and my sister's absences from school triggered the administration's machine and brought about repeated confrontations with its officials. I accompanied my mother to the Labor Inspection Office to follow up on my father's case. We haunted the corridors of town halls and social security offices. Mama sat in a chair, and I did my utmost to explain. Each person I spoke with gave me an endless amount of paperwork to complete. Each step required us to yet again prove our identity, our sources of income, and our home's maintenance. Then Mama would stand up with that absent-minded look she got when she faced things she didn't want to understand, refusing to see that the administration had the power to insinuate itself into our daily lives.

As for me, I saw shatter to pieces the illusion we entertained that we could be taken for people from here. That we could be looked upon lovingly by the Republic.

My father's boss claimed that the accident occurred outside of working hours, and he settled on paying a symbolic indemnity. All that remained was a small pension from my father's tragically early retirement.

My mother immediately stopped her trips to Alouane to cut back on our expenses. We absolutely had to have extra sources of income. I was fortunate to get a job as a secretary in a Corsican architect's office. I learned how to type. I answered the phone and swept every now and then when his cleaning lady was out. I went around thanking my colleagues for their kindness. Just like Papa.

"Will you stop thanking everyone! Where did you get that habit? You don't owe anyone a thing. Your boss doesn't allow you to live—your work does."

Geneviève was my work colleague. In her full thirties, rosy and smooth—like a real-life doll. With a Breton mother and an Alsatian father. She once gave me a headpiece from Colmar, and she regularly brought me Riesling, thinking that such a long time in France had opened my Muslim throat to alcohol. I didn't dare refuse. I gave the bottles to our building manager as a gift.

When I returned home from work, my mother had eaten and my sister had pretended to, but my father waited for me. He kissed my forehead and shared his meal with me. I was taking the steps recommended by the lawyer charged with defending him against his former boss. His fees had just swallowed up my first paychecks.

After dinner I wearily got up and pushed my father's chair over to the window, where he lost himself gazing out over Paris.

I found Amira in our bedroom. Lying on her bed, she stared up at the ceiling.

"Why don't you try to go out some? Get together with your friends from school. Go spend an afternoon with Noura and her kids."

"Noura?" she answered with a distant voice. "She stopped by today. She was shocked by my state. Not by the fact that I don't go to school anymore—her kids got her used to that idea—but by my *state.* As if she could understand anything about my state. I don't like that woman."

No more noises came from my parents' bedroom at night. All the same, I listened for Mama's laughter, a simple moan, a word spoken on the pillow. There was nothing anymore. Death roamed nearby. Despair was in Djamila's body. Across her longing for her country. And as a counterpoint to her hopes for the future.

My father died of a hemorrhage two years after his accident. I'm still convinced he had to have died from his wife's despair. He could no longer stand the silent reproaches that resided in Djamila's gaze or the folds of bitterness that the emptiness of her loveless nights had gouged into her cheeks.

We found him on a Friday night, his head in his wife's lap, the chair was upended not too far away.

Do you remember the day our father passed away, Amira? Listen to me; you never like to turn toward the past. I'm not telling you these things in order to stay alive like that crazy Scheherazade, but to kill time while waiting for the end. The storyteller from *One Thousand and One Nights* had reasons to stay alive. We only have reasons to die.

Do you think that the women—the young women back there, where we come from—dream of dying? No, I don't think so. They're filled with a passion for life, which I admire. They're fighting against time, misery, and their husbands' other wives. They think only about living, as though they enter the world anew each morning. And above all, they believe they must absorb it all so they can flourish. They would be shocked to hear that in the land of plenty we're destitute.

Only Grandmother guessed what France's sky had in store for us. But the younger ones, the city dwellers, the recent graduates? No. They envied our luck as emigrants. They would have gone about things differently than we had. Or at least they believed it was possible to do so.

When Béchir suggested that we have my father buried in Paris because of our financial difficulties, Mama threatened to kill herself. Never—not ever—would she leave him near the Infidels. While he was alive, she had tolerated this cohabitation, but she would give her life to keep him away from them in death. He would not make his journey up there in a parade of Jesus's children.

After thirteen years of exile, my mother got used to the imperatives of life in France but not to those of death. She really had little reason to worry about them. Muslims know that it is even harder to be let in when they die than it is when they are still alive. Some French people claim that Muslims' corpses are out of place among native ones. And that God might have trouble identifying his people.

We had to get the money to ship Papa's body back to Algeria. His old friends at the factory raised enough to partially cover the costs. Béchir organized the collection. I put in all my savings, and my mother provided the rest by selling three bracelets.

Papa—who had never liked flying—completed his final trip over the Mediterranean without fearing takeoff or saving up his sleeping pills and *surah*s from the Koran to self-administer at the gate on the rare occasion he didn't go back by boat. He had always assured us that once he was in the sky, he was fine. No would tell him, "You don't belong here." A true patriarch amid the flight crew and the hurried stewardesses. Served, spoiled, catered to. You'd think that he was right next to the good Lord on the stairs that lead to heaven. But alas, a quarter of an hour before landing, my father's anxiety and upset stomach would start again.

We made the trip with him and without him. He was boxed up in the baggage hold: one inanimate thing among others—a package of flesh between suitcases, folding chairs, strollers, Oriental rugs, plastic flowers, and diapers. My inert father, squeezed in between one thousand and one things amongst which he was one.

His friend Béchir drove us to the airport with a couple of compatriots—Papa's former colleagues. For the occasion, he put on the gray suit he wore for important events; it gave a hint of elegance to a body that was as slim as his wife Noura's was abundant. A new scarf blazed around her neck, matching the green eyes she'd inherited from her Kabylian family.

When it was time to depart, Béchir and his friends walked toward my mother. Their movements were solemn, their faces closed. They were no longer workers at Renault, anonymous immigrants, and fathers powerless to control their children. They had once again become the men from back home. Courageous and honorable—ready to protect the weakest, women and children.

"Fear not. We will always be at your side. May God protect you."

Their desire for Djamila, which had long ago been revealed in their eyes, made way for a new glint: one of pity and defiance.

They walked away, masculine and resolute until they passed through the sliding doors. Then the glacial cold at Orly bent their shoulders, and a few policemen's stares made them slow their steps.

As soon as Amira was back in Paris, she got into bed and refused to move. She claimed she was unable to sleep.

We had to call Béchir. Finding a shred of authority for the meeting, he threatened to send her back to Algeria if she continued being sick for no reason.

Amira gave him a vacant stare—it was impossible to tell the despair from the defiance. Their eyes, which were almost the same color, barely had time to meet. Béchir turned away, criticized my mother for her lack of firmness and demanded that she not give in to her daughter's whims, and then he left. That was the last time we would see him. He died a few days later of a heart attack. We figured it was because of the intensity he had on the day he reprimanded my sister—he had long since lost touch with his authority.

Amira, now back on her feet, agreed to follow my mother's orders and to go through the motions of daily life.

With my father gone, my mother decided that it was her duty to provide for the family. But there was some sort of perversion or indecency in her having to assume her husband's mantle. And she buckled under this obligation for which she was not prepared.

I still made minimum wage, and Amira, who got sick often, quickly managed to lose the internships I struggled to get for her.

Mama quit reprimanding Amira. But one morning she got up earlier than usual. She got dressed, covered her hair with a woolen hat, held a small bag against her stomach, and went out. She came back exhausted that evening. When she took off her shoes, I was surprised to see she had on my sister's sneakers. This detail seemed at once ridiculous and monstrous. I felt the same sense of consternation I had thirteen years earlier when

I saw her return home with her head uncovered. Djamila in sneakers. Something significant had to have gone through her mind to bring her to this—to place her other foot into "modernity." She had been forced to remove her veil. This new guise was no more desired than the first had been.

In the days that followed, Mama continued to go out at the same time in the same outfit. In the afternoon, she turned the key in the lock, came inside, and went straight to her bed, muttering, "I'm tired."

I begged her to eat and to talk. She refused and fell asleep in her clothes.

I imagine these were the days when she first started looking for work. She had the impression that she was begging. Lacerating Fattoum's body, which had been silent for so long. Baring her body and soul.

Women from her village had never worked, especially not in another woman's home. Until Mrs. Sentini's offer.

Much later, Mama told me about it. The wife of a small entrepreneur from Vanves lived in an opulent building with an elevator as big as a real bedroom. She took her time coming to the door. Looked my mother over from head to toe. Then she ran her hand over her permed hair, shook her watch, and said, "Good. You're on time."

She continued, "Do you know how to iron?"

"Yes."

"Cook?"

"Yes."

"But not just couscous. Pork roast, *tête de veau.*"

"I will learn."

Mrs. Sentini left Mama waiting on the doormat as she went to the large chest of drawers that took up a wall in the living room. Djamila caught a glimpse of the piece of furniture and told herself she had seen the same one last Sunday when she went by the Vanves flea market. She noticed that Mrs. Sentini was wearing rhinestone-encrusted mules.

"Here," Mrs. Sentini said, pressing two one-hundred-franc

bills into Mama's hand. "You'll get the rest at the end of the month. In cash."

And she turned and walked away, her hips swaying widely in her overly tight skirt.

That evening, we knew Mama's life had changed. We heard the bathroom faucets running well into the night. No matter how hard Pierrot pounded on the ceiling, Mama tried to ignore him. For the first time.

The next morning, we watched her fold her white apron and place it carefully into her plastic bag. Her movements were incredibly slow. She didn't dare look over at us. I knew better than Amira did that in a few moments, as Mama crossed the street, she would feel as if she were walking on her ancestors' bodies, on a past that distance had made even more glorious. She would desecrate the memory of so many proud uncles and women of strong character, and so many warriors and landowners. Djamila Bint Sidi Bou Ali, a maid for the French!

No one could console Mama like Latifa, the seamstress who declared that as far as she was concerned, "over there—it's done with!" and yet every summer she left for Tangiers via Spain with her husband and children all loaded up like donkeys. Here was a woman who knew how to convince others. This Moroccan woman was blessed with a rock-solid pragmatism that made her an excellent professor of affected humility.

"Don't play at being the grande dame, Djamila! Stop this charade of being the descendant of I don't know which marabout! You aren't going to be sending back photos of you scrubbing Mrs. Sentini's tile floors! You're not going to tell them about your real life!"

Little by little, Mama forced herself to conserve bathwater, to stop sighing so much, and to get used to working hard in order to bring home very little.

We set off once again with a new life: my mother was the cleaning lady, I was the secretary, and Amira played the role of the anorexic—everyone now acknowledged this.

"This is our fate," Mama said, more to console herself than to convince us of it. "We shouldn't complain too much. Allah wanted this! And if we're forced to live away from his home, we must make an effort to obey him in the foreigner's."

Anyway, it was out of the question to regularly go back to Allah's home—the trips to Alouane were too expensive. Yet we still had to visit my father's grave, and in spite of our meager incomes, we made the trip three years after his death.

Mama announced her plan to start shopping again. She was ready to burn through the savings that remained.

"I don't want the family or anyone else for that matter to suspect anything. There are so many jealous and envious people who'd be delighted to find out that we're naked."

"Who exactly are you thinking about?"

"Our old sharecroppers, your aunt Yvonne, who would have given everything to trade places with us . . . "

I interrupted her, demanding she not open her wallet for anything but the bare minimum. And she nodded. For some time now—in spite of the fact that she also worked—my mother didn't go against my wishes. She let herself be bossed around. I was far from being delighted with this role. I left without saying anything else, frightened by the heavy responsibility that fate had placed upon me and that perhaps foretold of serious hardship.

So we bought the bare minimum to maintain the villagers' esteem and our status over there. To prop up the myth. To seem.

Every morning in Alouane, my mother advised us on how we should look. I listened attentively. Amira nervously cracked her knuckles. Undoubtedly repressing an intense urge to vomit.

Mama rifled through the bottom of her suitcase and pulled out a handful of golden pins, costume jewelry, and lace hairpieces.

"What's all that junk?" grumbled my sister.

"Put this necklace on, and the pink hairpiece."

"I'll never go out wearing that. This stuff belongs in a carnival."

"*Carnafal* or no *carnafal,* you will go out with these on!"

Amira put on the dismayed look she wore each time Mama mangled her French. My sister pitied this language that was mashed between Mama's Swak-tinted gums as if it were a huge piece of chewing gum. I even bet she prayed that no other French speaker would ever hear Djamila's twisted words and invented expressions all pronounced with her villager's accent.

As our situation in France began to deteriorate, Mama and I felt the need to prove to the people of Alouane that our situation was really wonderful. I became an architect, and we created a diligent student's life for Amira.

"Oh, that's why she's so thin," commented Aunt Yvonne at lunch. "She must work night and day. Poor thing. In France, people feed themselves with diplomas," continued the woman who was still strongly attached to Roscoff. "You should have told us, Djamila. We were starting to worry about your daughter's health."

And she burst into laughter, showing her toothless mouth.

Amira quickly moved to the door. Once again, she went off to vomit away from watching eyes.

But my sister didn't come back. That afternoon I mentioned her absence to my mother. She was too busy introducing her sisters to French cuisine—she claimed to know its secrets. After barely one hour, the whole village had heard about the disappearance.

Relatives and friends gathered to look in courtyards and houses. A horde of kids was sent to check the nearby farms and search between hay bales and behind wheat silos. My aunt readied herself to call on Sadek the Mad's mother, the village fortuneteller.

It was a day in August. The sky suddenly filled with clouds, warning of one of those end-of-summer storms familiar to the plains of Souf. Then the clouds split open. A thick, heavy, seemingly enraged rain beat down upon the village. The new electrical lines were cut. Alouane's paths became streams. The *wadi* swelled within minutes.

A kid yelled. We saw two policemen from Alouane's new "security post" arrive; they were just as drenched as the rest of us were. They pushed through the crowd, each one holding on to one of Amira's wrists. She walked between them, her hair stuck to her face, trembling like a surprised animal caught in a deadly net.

"We fished her out of the *wadi,*" said one of the policemen. "She must not have realized how deep it was. She's not used to this."

Amira raised her head; her eyes met Mama's. The latter looked furtively away.

That evening, my mother fainted. They went out to find a young cousin visiting from Algiers; he had a car. He took her to Séra. The doctor concluded that it was simply emotional shock.

She avoided her daughter for a week.

For the whole visit, Mama and I wove together the fictitious plotline of our Parisian life with one lie after another.

With an indifferent and weary attitude, Amira listened to the stories we told half in French and half in Arabic.

"But you're lying!" she shouted on the first day.

"No!" asserted Djamila, fanatical. "This is what we have to do. Play the role of important people—of rich girls. My people love only appearances. And would give anything for you to be just as they imagine. If you were humbler or more modest, they would despise you. If you told them the truth, they would toss you aside as though you were filth. Never let them see your weakness, or they will finish you. Make them dream—they don't need the truth. They only need the soap opera."

And my mother was right. About these things, she knew what she was talking about. She knew her clanswomen and their passion for gossip all too well. She would not become their victim.

With superior force, I described the fine qualities of our neighborhood south of Paris, painting the island of dirty red-brick low-income housing projects squeezed in among hundreds of buildings that all looked alike as being a very corner in the garden of Eden.

I only mentioned our proximity to the beltway so that I could extol the magic of the capital's main arteries, where thousands of comfortable, fast cars traveled. I used the excessive number of tenants to create an image of the garden at Number 2 on the dead-end road of *impasse du Paradis* as being filled with ambitious and exuberant young people every evening. I convinced my female cousins that our spot on the sixth floor let us live in the clouds. I listed off the name brands in our closets and the French friends we'd never had, and I finished with an exhortation on the beauty and ease of living in France, the courteousness of its people, and the taste and flavors of its cuisine.

They looked at me in amazement. Especially the younger ones, who listened more attentively to me than they did the stories their grandmothers told them. I watched my sister's thin fingers; they trembled at times. She knew I was creating dreams, frustrations, and maybe a craze around me. But I couldn't have cared less. Something pushed me to hurt these people who were begging for false dreams. Who were consumers of occidental fictions.

A little later that evening, I sat in the middle of the large room where Grandfather used to receive visitors, and I did it again: I told stories about our trips to Alsace, our peregrinations on its wine route that led us to the château du Haut-Koenigsbourg—a name whose pronunciation alone granted me an even stronger aura in the eyes of my audience—and our stays in rural inns that were cozy, warm, and clean. I obviously got all of this from Geneviève.

I casually returned to talking about Paris, where the trees never lost their leaves, even in winter when the streets were lined with pines for the Christmas season. A holiday when the heavens opened for everyone—exactly like the Night of Ordainment for Muslims. Except that it rained real gifts. Religion and race didn't matter. You only had to lift a finger at a curve in the road, in a square, or in front of a church to make things appear: clothes, boxes of food, television sets, mattresses, washing machines, and other household appliances. Of course, I based this in part on the Restos du Coeur that had just opened up a mere two steps from our home.

Mama came to my aid, furthering the scene by speaking solely in her broken French.

"What you say, my dear? Come, that I hear better."

I saw my sister go red with shame. Mama persisted, however, determined to tell us what to do in this language that was not her mother tongue.

"Tell they, tell the blue tunnels at Bombidou and the vindows at department store Bon Marchi."

In such moments, our friends and relatives fell silent before the unfathomable mysteries Mama described. They were kept away from this immense privilege, frustrated at not being able to set foot—even symbolically—in the land of the ex-colonizer who for a century had delighted in boasting about the splendors of its kingdom without granting them entry.

Two years later, in 1990, during the second trip following my father's death, I couldn't go back over even the smallest thread of our tale. I felt this had something to do with my emotional health and my reflection, which I contemplated at some length in the well water.

Mama was less willing to speak in French and often sought refuge on her husband's grave. Afterward she would walk past her ancestor's *zaouia*.* Sometimes I surprised her there. She leaned over the tomb with the same posture as Grandmother Fattoum. From behind, she looked strangely like her. I thought to myself that perhaps my mother's life in France was only an illusion, a poorly sustained lie. And that in reality she'd always been here, in this position, riveted to the past.

She returned, sat on the patio, and stared at her ruined hands. Fattoum used to gather the peasant women to apply henna on her daughter's delicate amber-colored fingers. They would place a bowl of green powder at her feet, and for hours they decorated, they drew . . . Djamila, sitting on soft rugs, holding her palms out, asked them to draw small hearts or an eye with an escaping tear.

"What a notion," Fattoum commented, "a crying eye! May God protect us from misfortune."

Not one person in the village ever found out about the nature of our life in France or about the precariousness of our situation. The screen we had raised between reality and the villagers' imaginations remained solid. Their attention fell upon other new "zimmigrants." They stopped trying to determine the exact worth of our gifts and the number of bracelets Mama wore like they used to.

* Mausoleum.

In fact, it no longer took much effort or proof to convince the people of Alouane. No need for a big show. Nearly three decades of independence hadn't brought Algeria the prosperity promised by socialist slogans and military putsches. Quite the contrary. Year after year, the people of Alouane sank deeper into misery. They bestowed more prestige on those who came back loaded with big bags from the department store Tati than on those who were covered with diplomas, believing they could smell the fragrance of our supposed happiness in the cheap bottles of perfume we brought with us.

In their eyes, the simple fact that we lived in Europe kept us free from want and guaranteed our quality of life. The status of "resident in France" was comparable to stock market transactions: its value increased each time the Algerian economy tanked or the zealous faith of its Muslims threatened a resurgence. The two generally went together. Impoverishment combined with injustice emptied the fields and filled the mosques.

The mail we received from Algeria multiplied. Letters regularly arrived from the village and the surrounding area, the senders reminding us of who they were. Without ever actually saying so, they asked for small packages or the equivalent amount in francs. They mentioned our family ties and the obligation of hospitality commanded by the Prophet. Just in case . . . Everyone wrote to us at some time or another. Except for Grandfather Lazrag, who had been condemned to a two-fold suffering: the death of his wife and the confiscation of his lands.

I didn't understand what could have happened in order for the now independent Algerians to submit to having their freedom shackled and to injustices I believed similar to those that had justified their fight against the French occupants. I came into the world three years after the colonists left, and when I heard Cheikh Lazrag rail against a director of the agricultural cooperative, his words rang out as an enigma to me.

"You dare tell me that times were less forgiving during my youth! Independent Algeria isn't any gentler for its children than French Algeria was."

"What are you insinuating?" the man insolently responded. "We're free and sovereign. We've reclaimed our dignity and taught the entire world a lesson in heroism."

"One yoke has replaced the other," continued Grandfather as though he hadn't heard anything. "Socialism's face is no more humane than that of colonization."

"Algerians deserve the social well-being and justice they're yearning for. The country's wealth belongs to everyone. That's always been our motto. It does you no good to be bitter. Feudalism is done with!"

"Dictatorship after dictatorship," whispered Grandfather as though to himself. "Hatred after hatred, never staunched. Someday this abscess must burst."

Once back in France after this second trip, Mama was more unhappy than ever. Housekeeping ruined her health. She couldn't get over my father's absence, and she became less and less tolerant of her status as a maid. We understood her only too well: she passed pride down to us through her blood—she taught it to us through her gaze and her sighs, and on the rare occasions she talked about herself.

Only Mr. Zana, the Jew from Marrakech, had short conversations with her, on the rare occasions when she saw him. Those conversations revived her because a man had spoken with her, had asked for news about her family in Algeria, and had sighed while saying that it was time for the Jews' and Arabs' common God to put an end to their differences.

Mama had little interest in the Arab-Israeli conflict and contented herself with stealing glances at Mr. Zana's eyes. They held a permanent tear, like a cloud of softness or a glimmer of humanity. He always had a hello on the tip of his tongue; it rushed out as soon as someone appeared on the street corner. People rarely replied. Those who didn't know him stared at him as though he were crazy. Some responded by saying that they hadn't asked him for anything. Once, he was assaulted by a blind man he tried to help cross the street.

"Mind your own business! I didn't ask you to do anything, idiot!"

Mr. Zana got up without saying a word and started back toward the building, the cloud in his eyes dripping real tears.

We never dared ask Mama about going back to Algeria, even in the height of her pain. My sister and I couldn't envision this solution as being a balm that would soothe our wounds. Amira had few childhood memories there, and personally, I felt only a fleeting nostalgia for it. We each had our little France and the hope of survival here despite our growing solitude, our permanent concern for the future, Mama's prolonged silences, and her pain that grew deeper and deeper like the cracks Mrs. Sentini's cleaning products dug into her chapped hands.

She started complaining about the cold. Insisting that she was going to die from it. The worst thing, she said, was that it wasn't the same kind of cold as in Algeria—this cold was indifferent, haughty, and "foreign." A cold set into motion by an evil spirit's breath, blowing upward from a glacial hell that didn't appear in the purgatories foretold in the Koran.

She veiled herself once again. To keep warm, she said. But in spite of the scarf wound several times around her hair and neck and the long, faded green raincoat that fell to her heels, she shivered most of the time. The creaking of her bones replaced her laughter. We feared for her.

Without a doubt, this is what pulled Amira out of her lethargy. She found a position as a temp worker in a small accounting firm. And, with the strength of this resurrection we had no longer dared to hope for, she railed against our mother.

"Mama, you're not going to put us through your homesick meltdown now. 'A foreign cold!' Have you ever heard anything so irrational!"

"What I mean . . . "

"You want to go back home, right?" Amira cut in. "But what will you do with us over there? Lock us away at your parents' house? Marry us off to your cousins?"

"You don't know what you're talking about."

"And how will I get better," Amira continued, "in your country? It's horrified by the handicapped, mistreats the mad, and stones its women! No, I prefer the humiliation here to the way people are humiliated over there in your country. I was born here, and I want to stay. Here I can live in anonymity!"

My mother didn't understand the word *anonymity.* She simply responded, "What a dog's life!"

"A dog's life here is worth more than your human lives over there."

I hated you in that moment. For this disrespect of your mother. For this violence toward her. You'd forgotten the Prophet's adage that my father often repeated to us: "Paradise lies at your mothers' feet." But you'd been living through your hell for years, and you couldn't have had the slightest notion of paradise. And, I have to say it, in your anger, I was relieved to find the Amira we had believed was lost.

I know you would have liked to get rid of this Algeria that every jingle of your mother's bracelets brought back to you just as every one of your father's bows toward Mecca had long ago.

You'd have liked to have been born French, right? I know. Sometimes you half-confessed this to me. Unlike a lot of our compatriots who spend their time convincing themselves they're not French, you wanted—and perhaps this amounts to the same thing—to convince yourself that you were not Algerian.

On the fifth anniversary of Papa's death, Amira sought comfort in the arms of some guy named Nicolas. She was barely eighteen years old. He was twice that. He was an editor at a daily political paper. His militancy and his long diatribes against the privileged, the bosses, and the synarchists seduced her. Nicolas seemed so in love with grand principles and so concerned with the world's future that watching him once again gave Amira the desire to overcome her issues and her anorexia.

She managed to spend three months under his roof, pretending that her company had paid for her to go on a trip to the countryside. Several weeks were enough for her to realize that this king of ideas was merely a lowly courtesan. Every night, he came back very late, startling her from sleep and begging her to make him couscous. She threw up several times because she was anxious, and so she was slow to serve him; he called her lazy and brainless. One night, he shoved her onto the bed, vowing to punish her; he took her body with a savagery she didn't believe she could survive. Knowing nothing about vice, she cried from the pain when he would have preferred she cry from pleasure.

What an ironic fate! While my sister dreamed of one thing—to be French to the very tips of her toes—her Nicolas wished only to find an obedient Arab in her, a languorous *houri* who would yield to his whims and satisfy his fantasies. Even in the worst of our harems from long ago, I don't think our women had to submit to these perverse acts of love.

This was likely when Amira became fully aware that the metamorphosis she'd desired for so long was impossible. No, she could not have a different body, nor could she change her destiny. Beneath Amira's white skin, Djamila's blood continued to flow. Despite Amira's complicity with her French friends, her sister would always be named Nacéra. Her illness probably stemmed from this pain. Her fits of crying, her refusal to eat, and those prolonged fasts that paradoxically ended the moment when the month of Ramadan began.

To fall so low. To be this ashamed of us? Always making fun of my black curls: "They're signs of underdevelopment and barbarism. The opposite of refinement and modernity," you said. "Shut up," interrupted my mother. "In other places, this lioness's mane would carry Nacéra to a throne." "Sure, a card-board one!" you shouted before fleeing to our room.

You don't exist, my sister—you don't exist for these people. Only the idea they have about you exists. No matter how you look, they'll judge you by your name. All the Amira that you are, you will be like me—a halo of frizzy hair. Now do you understand that you're not French? You're shaking your head. How can you not agree? Who are you then? You idiot! And in what state of delusion were you calling yourself Marie!

And who am I with you? At more than thirty years old? I can only see myself in your eyes. I can't do without you.

One night, Amira came home with a swollen face and strands of hair ripped out from her head. When I opened the door, I saw a young man with her. He was in his thirties with a tall frame and nearly yellow eyes. A compatriot who had picked her up at a metro station where she'd had a very close call.

A young black girl had asked Amira to get out of her seat. Amira crudely refused. The black girl grabbed her by the throat. In vain, my sister tried to defend herself.

"You filthy black, go back home!" she yelled.

"It's you who should get out of this country, you filthy sand monkey! This is my home."

"Nigger, one look at you is enough to see that I'm more French than you. You hear me! More French than you!"

And she offered up her face to the scratches and punches that beat down upon her.

Not one passenger stirred. After all, this didn't have anything to do with them. Only the boy got up to defend her. The other girl was pushing her toward the tracks, and Amira was letting it happen.

When the young man described the scene, we saw Mama break down in tears for the very first time; her eyes were drowned in humiliation. She cried for a long time. A long time.

The breakup with Nicolas was official, and Amira moved back into our apartment. With nothing to do, she wandered the neighborhood during the day and withdrew into her room at night without speaking to us. She would, however, assail the shopkeepers and neighbors. She hounded Pierrot. Every time she passed by him, she muttered insults in poor Arabic. She called him "pig" and "fag." Eventually, he came up to complain to my mother.

But she came home so exhausted from housekeeping, and

she so feared her daughter's mood swings that she didn't even have the strength to reprimand her.

Once again, Amira refused to take in the smallest bit of food. After three days, Mama ventured opening up to Mrs. Sentini about it.

"She doesn't want to eat? It's nothing. All young girls her age want to look like the fleshless models featured in women's magazines. The editors of these publications are criminals. They should be put on trial."

On her way home, Mama bought a *Marie-Claire* and flipped through it, horrified. How could girls this thin ever hope to please?

As soon as Mama walked through the door, she went over to Amira and threw the magazine onto her lap.

"What they tell me must be true. You're not sick like the doctor says. You read this garbage in secret, and you want to look like these walking skeletons! I always thought God created you to punish me."

Did Mama really believe Mrs. Sentini's explanation, or was she trying to secure a glimmer of hope?

"If it's true that you're not truly sick, it's because you're my daughter by mistake," she added.

"Try to understand. Your sister's illness is a way of trying to find her place, to fight, to look as though she is from this country. Has she ever attempted suicide?"

I recoiled from the question. "Never."

"How strange!"

This was what my friend Geneviève's fiancé, Jean-Louis, said to me one day. He was a resident at the Salpêtrière Hospital. He was the only one in whom I confided my concerns about my sister.

"In a way, your sister's treating one illness with another."

So that was it. All of Amira's resentment toward a country that nobody wanted to say was hers and that despised her father, her resentment toward the exile that tattooed her mother's hands with cleaning products—she expressed this by refusing to eat. When she insulted Pierrot, it was vengeance for the meager love France had for her and for the little space it granted her.

In the end, she was the most Algerian of all of us. What was this paradox? Neither our parents nor I wanted to rebel against our adoptive country. We were just trying our best to find a place here. To spend our days here in peace. But with Amira, it was different. Because she was born here.

Jean-Louis also thought my sister knew how to see better than we did. She had seen the impasse. She no longer wanted to spend time with people her own age. She no longer considered us worth talking to about her agony. She didn't know her native culture and language well enough to seek refuge in it. And France didn't open its arms to her. Everything made her sick. Her parents' past and her own future.

Without thinking, I asked, "And what if she were a boy?"

"She probably would have blown off steam by beating up whites, setting cars on fire, and smashing in storefronts. She would have cried racism. But, while others her age are expressing themselves through violence, she has shut herself off. She preferred to give up."

From time to time, Amira did stir from her torpor long enough to find temp work. But she quickly became discouraged, said she was always exhausted, and let herself be fired . . .

In 1992, the crisis broke out in Algeria. The bearded ones intended to take on the role of the ancestors and dictate their laws. News arrived, ever more alarming and tragic. They raped women. They strangled old men. They tore the limbs from children and cut off their heads while facing Mecca, following the same rituals required for the slaughter of sheep during Eid.

They spread terror in my mother's small village, where no such barbarism had ever before entered. My aunts' daughters called us expressly to ask for help, begging for just a corner of a mattress so that they might have nights without knives—under exile's sky, but under one more clement than that of a country that was now foreign to its children. May God forgive them—they didn't know what they were asking of three destitute women! Their story was certainly dire, but so was ours.

My mother abandoned her desire to return, a desire she'd been nurturing without telling us. She was afraid we would have our throats slit. Three women guilty of having lived alone in a hated land. We were condemned in advance. And so, for the time being, at least, we were forbidden to return.

One day, I found among the letters that came from Alouane a page ripped from a school notebook: *Whatever you do, don't come back. There's a rumor going around that your grandfather Lazrag had connections with the* harkis, *and the only reason that he didn't have his land taken away during colonization was because he helped the French. I don't know the source of this insult. If you dare return, they will show you no pity.*

This faceless *they* became our judges. Their imprecise identity made them even more monstrous; the unpredictability of their aggression heightened the terror they spread; the arbitrary nature of their cruelty underscored our weakness. From then on, there was an unbeatable foe more terrible than fairy-tale ogres, more abominable than the Chitane,* and even more terrifying because this foe had a human name.

Mama cried, losing all sense of reason, on the day when a phone call informed her that her uncle was dead, his throat slit by a former sharecropper.

"Slimane, the son of Kaddour, our old sharecropper," sobbed her oldest sister, "it was him."

Within the space of a second, I remembered the young boy bent over between my cousin Myriam's legs.

"But why? Why?" cried Mama.

The line went dead. My mother tried again, night after night, to get an answer. She didn't get one. Slimane was the shiest and the most solitary of their old sharecroppers' children. We barely knew his voice, and he always walked with his eyes lowered like the women. It was thought that his reserve was the result of a childhood trauma: his father had been found dead, his body thrown in a well.

Then other news came. Baroudia, Mama's niece, raped by a rejected suitor. Her brother killed on the road to Alouane as he was coming back from the university in Algiers to spend a few days with his already grief-stricken family.

Not one of us could understand so much hatred; it was like a thirst for a long-suppressed revenge. All the years of injustice and rancor and the tyranny Grandfather talked about exploded like an abscess. And like a deep hunger for sex. A hunger among this people whose sharp divisions seemed to feed off of a very powerful, subterranean fire of carnal obsessions. Off of the bodily hauntings of all the Djamilas.

Then Mama started calling late at night. She probably hoped that the reality as well as the nightmares would dilute into the fringes of the night. They listed off the victims' names. They told her about their martyrdom. They described the young boys who spread terror in the village. Often these boys returned from the capital after years of aimlessness and unemployment; they arrived in Alouane with their load of resentment, heavy with

* Satan.

the hatred inherited from past generations. Sometimes she could place the names. Others she didn't know.

"Boors," declared one of my cousins, who had become a professor in Séra. "Those excluded from knowledge, the illiterate, weak, and misogynistic: there you have Alouane's new masters."

And the cousin hung up in tears.

This is when Mama started talking about her country. Not about herself—she never allowed herself to do that—but about her country. Out surged its vast lands and its villages set between plains and mountains. Its capital, which she had visited for the first time when she took the boat to Marseilles. Algiers the White, perched on the sea as if to better hide its secret. Algiers, which had astonished her with its serene solemnity, its virile winds, its nights full of the salty smell of seaweed. She had climbed the steps of the narrow streets that snaked all the way through the Casbah amid the noise of the roaming merchants and the *youyou*s of the mothers celebrating their young boys' circumcisions. Then, farther away toward the east—almost on the Tunisian border—the memory of her village began: its green valleys where children played without fear like young lambs that Providence protected from the wolves.

Where did such eloquence come from? She had always expressed herself through her body rather than words. Had she been possessed by her ancestors' poetry? When I listened to her, I thought about the victims of strange breakdowns who, in the middle of their suffering, begin to speak in languages they'd never heard. Her longing for Algeria filled her with this ability. Then her eyes, red from crying, closed upon the old images of happiness. She fell asleep. Or pretended to.

I then grasped how much this country meant to her. Fifteen days in Alouane could make her forget her life as a cleaning lady and restore her dignity. Across the Mediterranean, she became a complete person again. A few steps in the airport in Algiers were enough for her to rediscover, through the desire in men's eyes, that she was still a woman.

The country's doors had just closed. Impossible to go back without running the risk of never returning. The very thought of this left Mama gasping for air.

"Open the windows—I feel like I'm going to die!"

Yes, she started wishing for death. Mama, her husband's widow and now her country's widow as well.

As her daughters, we felt like this land's orphans as soon as we were prohibited from returning. The minute tragedy took Algeria away from us, Algeria became our motherland. The intensified memories of Alouane tormented us, leaving us with the bitterness of impossible reunions. The past turned its back on us, and yet it dragged us along behind it.

Though we believed we'd inherited so little from our parents, their silence had ultimately forged this country within us. Why must clarity be found on the flip side of hardship?

We stayed glued to the television news and to the rare programs devoted to the "events." Through the news professionals, we discovered the consummate art of the euphemism. The scenes always opened on a recent bomb explosion. Sometimes we heard the crackle of gunfire. We saw streams of blood in the streets. A mattress and two battered suitcases. A cluster of crushed tomatoes. A single plastic boot. A diaper next to a well.

Then the correspondent, deciding to stop at the very limit of what could be shown, moved on to another topic. We had the impression that Algeria was erasing itself. Everyday life apparently didn't interest the joyless reporters. We channel surfed from one tale of sadness to the next with gaps and silences perfectly matching this Algeria that still lived in spite of everything; news about this Algeria might have comforted us.

So, through a strange sort of mimicry, we convinced ourselves we were also in danger. Why? It was so easy to substitute Algeria for France in our minds—I suppose just like over there where so many Algerians confused their country with that of the French.

We got into the habit of scrutinizing everything around us, of suspecting our neighbors and passing strangers, stairwells and trash cans, ringing phones and the sound of irregular steps. At night, we double bolted the door, just like our neighbor Rose.

When attacks were carried out in France in 1995, our fear of the fundamentalists grew to include the fear our French hosts inspired in us. We worried we would look like terrorists and become victims of acts of revenge.

We hid out of fear of being disemboweled. We lowered our eyes more than the women back there. We walked close to walls and apologized, silently apologized for everything we hadn't done, for each breath of air, each corner of sky, each crumb of bread, each seat on the metro, each cent given us by the French.

I had to comfort Mama. Over her homesickness, her fear of never again seeing her plains that would one day turn green. I had to help her with her migraines, bandage her ruined hands, and scrub her back for a long time while she was in the bath.

No one came to visit her. Except for Mr. Zana, who stopped by from time to time to see if there was news from over there. Our few Algerian friends lived too far away. They were also worried about the tragedy, and we saw no sign of them. For our part, we made no effort to reconnect with them and found all sorts of excuses for not going to visit.

After Béchir's death, Noura signed up for her neighborhood mothers association. She intended to succeed where her husband had failed and bring her children back onto the right path. The *harki*'s wife suddenly lifted her chin. Cinched up in tight pants and a red shirt, her belly was less prominent now since she had lost her husband; this made her look a few years younger, and, for the first time, she took in some of her family members whom the war had thrown onto her doorstep with neither luggage nor regrets. Noura opened her door to them and went out the next day to mollify the members of her association. It was necessary to intercede, to find housing and work for the newly exiled. Of course they all had diplomas, and a little while ago they were leading a different kind of life. But they shouldn't be choosy. "It's better to wax floors or be a parking lot attendant in peace than to be in charge of major operations over there, under terror," she consoled her compatriots who had only just arrived.

"If only we had clear reasons to act or demand rights," Amira sometimes said with cynicism. "It wouldn't matter which ones. We don't even have a brother who was gunned down by the cops by mistake. Shoved into the Seine out of contempt.

We would have benefited from solidarity, even here with the French."

I didn't reply, but I silently took over in the same way a bird's wing naturally rises after the other.

A father lost to a banal accident. A mother aching for her country. A life without joy. Amira's anorexic crises. Moneyless, like all poor people. Nothing that could allow hope.

"No one worries about those who ask for nothing," my sister continued in a quiet voice. "And those are the ones who are wrong. The real evil is there. And it will kill us."

She spoke through allusions and aphorisms. And even if I didn't always grasp what she was saying, I knew her mouth loathed everything except the truth.

It was to be expected. Prematurely aged, depressed, weakened—Mama couldn't continue cleaning Mrs. Sentini's home.

With relief, she cloistered herself at home and spent her days walking through the three rooms or napping on her sheepskin. Sometimes she'd stay at the window. Rose walked through the building's courtyard wearing a gray dress and a hat in both summer and winter; she must have inherited them from a grandmother. Rose didn't make a sound. She went through life in silence, focused on her flower boxes and her mail. Never a man with her. Single like us, and she seemed to know how to get by. She never made any noise apart from that of her key in the door twice a day and the clinking in her cash register at the supermarket. Back when Mama did her shopping there, Rose pretended not to know her, double-checking the items and prices, as if a woman named Djamila would absolutely try to trick her.

My mother no longer showed herself. If a neighbor asked how she was doing, I gave a vague reply. That said, after the news of a massacre that left twenty dead in Alouane, Pierrot came up out of concern to see if she needed anything. Mama thanked him coldly and didn't invite him in.

There had to be Algerian victims to make a good neighbor out of Pierrot. Amira said that they liked us either dead or martyred. The passport stamped with pain or nothing. To make people feel sympathy in order to exist.

Once Pierrot was gone, Mama said, "I don't see Mr. Zana around anymore. I hope nothing has happened to him."

And she became quiet, her eyes lost in space.

Amira, who now worked in one of Mr. Sentini's blown-glass companies, complained about the close quarters at work. Working at reception or at the phones, she was the only woman, isolated in a miniscule office across from the workshop and the furnaces. When a worker or a courier walked in, she blatantly looked away, quickly discouraging them from any further attempts. Only the boss would sometimes get through the door to ask about her work. She thought he gave her filthy and suspicious looks, and she answered him in monosyllables, going into detail only if he insisted.

We begged her not to antagonize him, to be mindful of this opportunity, and to keep this job she owed to the Sentinis' extreme kindness. To this, she usually responded with contempt, turning her back on our pleas and shutting herself in her room.

A few weeks later, we weren't surprised when Amira smirked as she told us that she wouldn't be going back to her job. She had slapped the boss. She didn't pretend to be looking for another job. And I had neither the time nor the heart to find another one for her.

Able-bodied, she settled into Papa's old wheelchair. She caressed its wheels at length and watched my mother, spinning Papa's beret around on her index finger in front of her eyes. Mama sat on her sheepskin, her fingers endlessly pressing into her blue tattoos. They didn't speak. Djamila with her spirit wandering in Alouane, her daughter in the middle of a prison without borders. But the same murdered hope lived in their motionless bodies.

When I came home, Mama struggled to get up. She reheated some pasta or some leftover ragout and then left to go lie down. I tried to share a bit of bread or a spoonful of semolina with my sister. She refused. I threatened to call over a doctor. She suddenly stood and followed our mother, seeking refuge in her bed. I was alone.

I thought about Papa watching the smoke rising out of Paris's chimneys. And about the miracle that would save us.

Up to that point, I hadn't lived. And when this boy introduced himself, I forgot my mother's prolonged silences, my sister's crises, and our money troubles.

I bought myself a black dress and earrings from Bon Marché. Shoes that cost a third of my paycheck and that I had to take off on the stairs so as not to shock Mama and Amira. My purchases were an insult to our growing misery, to Amira's anguish, and to the hardship of the Algerians who remained over there. I knew I had to experience all of this as a luxury, but this time I wanted to push from my mind the idea that I had no other purpose than suffering.

Adel brought the first ray of light into my life. He was the one who had brought Amira back the day of the metro fight two years back. We had crossed paths by chance in the Montparnasse neighborhood. I didn't have any trouble recognizing him. And I knew he recognized me because he gave me a complicit smile. He asked me out for coffee. We saw each other again one week later.

The first night, he looked at my dress without saying anything. He came from a place where affairs of the heart were placed above matters of taste; he didn't expect me to spend so much money to please him. He was the oldest of six children and came from a family that had stayed in Algeria, and he said he had come to Paris in hopes of finding work and escaping barbarism. He had only managed to get odd jobs that were poorly paid and always under the table.

Thin, aquiline nose, very white skin—he reminded me of my sister.

He walked by my side, rarely taking my hand in public, giving me orders when we were with his friends. As soon as we found ourselves alone in his studio apartment—just a few square meters and right in the middle of the outer suburbs—he changed completely. He gently kissed me on the forehead, slowly caressed my hair, whispered such sweet words that I ended up believing I'd been wrong about Arabs. I thought they were tough and macho. They were tender like children.

Sometimes Adel put his head between my breasts and wept. I asked why. He didn't answer. I noticed that he was often on guard in the street, worried and anxious. He reassured me that this was merely his temperament.

We were together for more than a year. I would rush over to his place as soon as I finished work.

I gave him my body as an offering—it had never belonged to anyone else. I ran my hand over his mole-speckled skin. I wanted to give him everything he needed. To chase away his anguish and his tears. To gently rock him. I wanted to be his wife, his sister, his Algeria, and his France all at once. And he disappeared.

I don't know how. For the first time ever, he didn't come to meet me. I waited late into the night, and then I went home. I told myself I had gotten the day wrong and went back the next day to the same place, at the same time. In vain. I decided to go by his studio. The door was closed. It remained so for the weeks and months that followed.

I started looking for the few people I'd ever seen in Adel's company. I wandered through the suburbs, both near and far and without a precise destination, asking idle kids if they'd seen a young man with white skin and an aquiline nose.

At night I went back to my lonely bed and bit my pillows so I wouldn't scream. Adel's disappearance stole away my interest in work. At the office, they pointed out my coming in late, my distractedness, and the files I misplaced. The boss came to the definitive conclusion that it was impossible for Arabs to work seriously on a task and told me to go join one of my cousin's harems. I had worked in his firm for nearly ten years. Why had he waited so long to share with me his opinion of Arabs?

With Geneviève by my side, I said my goodbyes to my colleagues one by one. I would have thanked them for everything, but my friend's scowl dissuaded me. Only she had gotten me a farewell gift.

I didn't want to break Mama's heart by telling her I'd been fired for cause. Hopeless, I wandered around for entire days. I went through the National Employment Agency's job centers to try to find work, then to the Labor Inspection Office. I even ventured into hospitals, taken once more by my old dream of becoming a nurse, hoping to find a little job where I could wear a white uniform.

There was an offer to fill in at the supermarket. I refused, disgusted at the thought of our neighbors seeing me behind the cash register like Rose. I was hired by a real estate agency in the 15th arrondissement. I couldn't manage to rent or sell a single square meter, having neither the talent nor the energy to persuade the clients.

At the National Employment Agency, they reproached me

for my bad attitude. I slammed the door on the way out. I ended up convincing myself that no one would find me good enough for a position in a company and that I should be looking in the classifieds.

I plucked out the babysitting ads and kept an eye out for positions in clothing stores. These jobs hardly lasted more than a few weeks. But they helped me sustain my household; I mechanically ensured its upkeep while staying away from its ghosts.

Again and again I wandered, the thought of going home giving me chills. My feet often led me back to Montparnasse.

Once, I collapsed on a bench in the metro station, exhausted. Nearby vagrants shot me funny looks. One of them came over and offered me a cigarette. I politely refused and got up.

A voice whispered: "What are you doing, Nacéra? How can you let this happen? You, your mother's daughter. Her ancestors are so respected over there. How can you fall so low?"

So I went back up the escalator and walked to our building. I saw Pierrot.

"I don't see your mother or your sister anymore."

I lowered my head, unable to give him a response.

"What a family! Half invisible—half mute. When I say that foreigners are strange . . . " grumbled our neighbor as he walked away.

The next day, a letter arrived from Algiers, along with the others. We kept receiving them and feared opening them, knowing that every request our people made would be in vain—every appeal for help had no hope of a reply. This time, the letter was personally addressed to me. A cramp seized my stomach when my eyes fell on the sender's name.

I left against my will. This is often how it goes for those who don't have papers in your *country and who don't always manage to escape the police's net. I was chased down like a piece of filth. Now I'm risking everything—that is certain. But there's no torture more deeply cruel than that of a man who is tied up and sent back to his people defeated and on his knees. I loved France; I have learned once and for all that it didn't love me. But for me this has been like discovering our independence for a second time . . . I didn't dare tell you I'd been living without papers for months because I was afraid you'd misunderstand my intentions. Circumstances have separated us. But you never know. Maybe one day Algeria will reunite us.*

Salutations. Phone number. Wrong one.

For many nights I had the same dream: A rental car drives along the road to Alouane. Adel is one of its passengers. Out comes an armed gang. A fake checkpoint. With wooden staffs and the butts of their guns they force everyone to get out. Six men and one old woman. They line them up against a row of Barbary fig trees. Only the old woman has the courage to break rank. She rips open the front of her dress and reveals her withered chest.

"Go ahead—kill the ones who gave you life! Make the blood of the breast that gave you milk run! You vile creatures—you cowards, you only attack those who are weaker than you! If there's a God, you'll be the first ones he throws into the pit of he . . . "

She doesn't have time to finish. The blade that slits her throat freezes her mouth around the final letters. The five other heads follow. My beloved's is one of them.

Mama and Amira, prostrate and absent, knew about my professional disaster; they didn't know about my heart's tragedy.

Like them, I no longer had a taste for living. We lived in three separate homes within the same apartment, each of us enclosed in our own solitude and tragedy. Our own aching.

I entered into their silence. I made my footsteps on the stairs and in our apartment scarce. A few errands and some shoddy tidying up were enough for us. Only the cat complained if I waited too long to give him his pittance. We never had visitors. No one dreamed of coming to talk with us. Our neighbors no doubt asked themselves what could be going on in the apartment of the three cloistered women. We avoided running into them, let alone saying hello. They didn't say hello, either.

What were we expecting? How would we live? And on what? Not one of us explicitly asked these questions.

A few months after Adel's letter, Mama died.

The final days of her life were spent in total silence. She took a couple of steps around the apartment, and going against habit, she opened the windows wide. She leaned out over the courtyard where stray grass was growing. Whenever a face looked up at her, she came back in, returning to her spot where she slowly carded her fingernails through the sheepskin, on which there was no more wool than hair on a balding skull. She sat back down. Oddly, her two remaining bracelets no longer clinked together.

She watched Amira. She lost herself in the sight of her daughter's body and seemed to count the protruding bones one by one. My sister's thinness probably inflicted upon her evidence of a failure she no longer dared admit to herself. Amira's white skin was proof of a betrayal whose nature she couldn't identify.

One morning she took a hard fall while she was holding herself up near the window. The doctor told us she suffered from a serious illness. He didn't say which one—he simply added, "It's time to think about your daughters' future."

I thought back to her first fainting spell in Alouane on the day Amira had been rescued from the floodwaters.

The diagnosis didn't seem to surprise my mother. I tried hard to guess what she was thinking. Her nostalgia, chased off with bursts of constrained laughter, had paved the way for the affliction. Her love of Algeria, relegated to the depths of her being, had poisoned her body. She'd been a traitor to the point of forcing her mother tongue to take the *roumi*'s tongue as its concubine.

And then our mother died out of her desire to pass away

before you did, Amira. Because she knew you were condemned. Just as she probably knew I couldn't live without the two of you.

"It's time to think about your daughters' future," the doctor insisted.

We couldn't find anyone to help us take her body back over there. Our group of compatriots had long since disappeared. Mama didn't leave any instructions regarding her final resting place. She knew our money troubles all too well to create new ones for us. Maybe she hated Allah's cemeteries because they were overflowing with murdered women and children.

She might even have wanted to punish herself by accepting what she had protected my father against: being buried far from her home, in Christian soil.

I took the necessary steps to get the burial permit and managed to get her a small plot in a Muslim cemetery near Paris. We were alone with Geneviève at the burial. Then Geneviève said her goodbyes. She was moving to Alsace-Lorraine; she was going back to her people with Jean-Louis, who was opening his psychoanalyst office.

We didn't cry that night. The pain was too great. And your body was so spent and so dry that it could have been wrung out and still not have yielded a single tear.

Amira, do you know that that night I dreamed about a glimpse of sun, back alleys, and poverty among my people? The luxury of misery over there.

Our mother didn't want that. Not out of fear for our lives but out of fear of disappointing her people. Rather than return empty-handed, Mama preferred to die. She chose to have news of her death rather than news of her ruin make it back over there. She accepted being buried here. Rather than having to admit to the lies she had maintained for all of these years.

I put Mama's old apron in my bag and went to knock on Mrs. Sentini's door. She didn't seem surprised to see me, but she didn't invite me in. She told me she was very busy and couldn't talk long. An urgent meeting. "A date," she added before I had even opened my mouth. She'd just hired a Romanian named Eva; she was very satisfied with her. It was too late. Well, maybe someday . . . Goodbye. She didn't even ask how her old cleaning lady was doing.

From that point on, I found only odd jobs doing caretaking work, selling things at markets, or handing out flyers on the street.

Businesses and offices would have liked to consider me, but they noted my lack of education, training, and knowledge of European languages. No one dared look me in the eye and explain my principal handicap: my name was Nacéra Touirellil.

Geneviève called me every now then and advised me to get more serious about "taking action." "Why are you not writing to the mayor, to the social benefits office, to local officials, even to the president himself? Harass them! These are your rights and your father's. Demand them already!"

But I was no longer armed for such steps. Like Mama in her time, I would have felt as though I were lowering myself to begging . . . The very thought of it gave me chills. I trembled at the thought of being looked down upon by the people at social services. I hated the thought of answering questions, of clearing up the mystery of the bills and final notices, of providing references who could vouch for my honesty.

In fact, I hated asking—that's all. This was when I realized that this was maybe the most discreet—yet the most real—

legacy passed down from my Algerian parents. Out of pride, I could never demand, solicit, or argue—even with anonymous parties.

I know Rose spends a large part of her time writing letters. I often see her going to the post office before showing up at the supermarket. I only need to look at the mail filling her mailbox, which she tirelessly answers by mailing back checks, subscriptions, bank statements, forms for automatic withdrawals, long letters of complaint, lists of calculation errors, serious points of outrage, apologies . . .

Rose likes to ask things of the state, to blame it, to hold it accountable—it's as if she were addressing a living person. As for me, I couldn't do it.

My sister and I had become second-class citizens. Pushed to life's underbelly. We had spent all of our savings. We had no more resources—no friends to lend us money.

The bills piled up. Rent, water, electricity, my mother's burial fees. I saw the final notices sticking out of the mailbox, and I didn't take them out. What for? After the electricity, they were probably going to cut off the water.

That was when I started selling the things in our apartment. I started with the radio, then the television, and then the empty suitcases left behind from Mama's old love of shopping. A few days later I had a vendor from the Vanves flea market come up so I could sell him my mother's bed, the kitchen table, and the two fake leather armchairs.

Only our bedroom remained intact. Blankets and mattresses were necessary for this harsh start to winter.

Pierrot saw me taking objects one by one out of the apartment. He contented himself with a sigh.

Everyone else had shut the door in our face. Politely. Conscientiously. Sometimes involuntarily. I think about him, Adel, who never tried to get back in touch with me. I wait in vain for him to call. That was my last ray of hope. Without it, Amira, I would have pushed you along with me in spite of you—in spite of everything—to return to Algeria.

We're alone. Not one familiar voice has come through our door in three months. No calls. We hardly ever go out anymore. We live on what we got for the sale of our personal effects. Amira, I see you getting thinner before my eyes. Digging your grave without complaint.

Our windows have been closed for a long time. I don't know if it's day or night. But I hear footsteps. It can't be very late. Who do you think is coming up? I'm asking you, Amira, but you're too far from me. You don't answer me. It's Rose, our neighbor across the hall. She usually turns her key at nine o'clock at night once the supermarket has closed.

Do you think our neighbors will try to find out how we are doing? I suspect they're relieved not to be seeing me anymore. Especially now as they look away from my shadow skimming along the walls of the stairwell.

Only Pierrot braved nearing me one more time.

"Have you seen the state you're in? Really, there are doctors and social services in this country! Why aren't you looking for work to get by? At your age, you're far from being unable to work. Go to the National Employment Agency! Ask for unemployment—it's made for people like you."

". . ."

"I don't understand! You're refusing all help for no reason. You lock yourself inside even when no one wants to hurt you. And afterward, people will say that people die of misery in France. They'll even say it's because of racism that we let you perish. Is that what you want? It is, isn't it?" he repeated, leaving me in front of the building's doorway.

At night, I cried for a long time in the kitchen, right next to Papa's wheelchair no one wanted to buy.

Your birthday was three weeks ago. I would have liked to have seen you upright, to wash your dry skin, to fix up your foul-smelling hair. Neither of us had the courage to talk about it. It would have sounded like a terrible farce. You came into your twenty-sixth year with the weight of a child and the cynicism of an old man. You greeted the most beautiful time of your life with a firm desire to be done with it.

I managed to convince you to see a doctor just one time. I promised you I would ask nothing else of you after that. You agreed to go with me.

I was lucky to find an old iron on a bathroom shelf. It took me a while to go down the six flights. I went over to the young Moroccan's grocery store. His father was there. He mumbled a Muslim saying to drive away spirits: "May God protect us from the devil!" I begged his son to trade us a few cans of food for the iron. Watching me leave, he grumbled: "I knew it. Harems without a male bring bad luck."

I helped you walk to the nearest hospital.

"Your sister is in serious condition," said the doctor. "We need to keep her here."

"Never!" I answered.

"Why?"

He didn't get an answer. I would have had to admit that I couldn't be away from you—that leaving you would untie me from the other half of my body.

"Then sign the discharge papers. If something happens to your sister, you'll be responsible. Not us."

I set it in writing: *I refuse to hospitalize my sister.*

He lectured me before leaving: "You should take care of yourself, too. You're frightening to look at. And take a bath. You'll feel better."

I wrapped my arm around your waist, and you leaned your thin body against my shoulder. We came home together for the last time. Two ghosts in broad daylight.

Do you know what I saw written on our door when we came back from the hospital? "Caution! AIDS!" You see, Amira, in our neighbors' eyes, we're the incarnation of evil. All we have to do is step foot outside and we bring back STDs. Because we're young, the only thing we can succumb to is excess.

I know the author of these words hanging on our door. It was Pierrot's son. Everyone in the building knows he belongs to an extremist group, and he's committed to making us hate this country. Oh, no, it wouldn't be his father. Pierrot is too impatient. His hatred is too spontaneous to form into a speech or a strategy. His lack of discipline is too significant to accommodate strict orders.

That time I sat down near the vagrants in the Montparnasse metro station, I saw his son. He was with a dozen or so skinheads, their elbows and knees covered with studded leather, lying in wait for the dark skinned. He didn't notice me. Or he pretended not to.

From the window I don't see the two lesbians walking by anymore; they spared us pitying smiles. As though we shared a secret or a stain with them. Mr. Zana came back. He came to see us with a basket from the country, which he placed on the kitchen table. He made soup and lemon chicken. He didn't comment upon our alarming appearance, the bareness of our apartment, or the candles we used for light.

"Eat, my girls. You need it. Your sadness will not bring back the ones you've lost."

He added, visibly worried, "I was gone for too long. A family situation to take care of. I didn't know that . . . "

Embarrassed, he continued, "I won't be able to come and see you anymore. I am leaving for Israel."

I smiled to reassure him, but I couldn't help asking, "Why Israel? What about Morocco?"

"I am too old to chase after a passion. I am going to see if it is good to die somewhere else."

I suppose he was the one who alerted the social worker to our state before he left.

The apartment buzzer went off again. It took me a long time to shake my lethargy. But this morning I had eaten the rest of the soup Mr. Zana brought. As the heat had been cut off, the soup had stayed somewhat fresh. I managed to open the door.

The woman introduced herself, and I jumped, because, Amira, you yelled, "We're not beggars! We aren't asking for charity from anyone!"

You stood behind me. By what miracle had you gathered enough energy to follow me? Amira, your eyes glittered with hatred.

The social worker stayed calm. She didn't comment. But she tried again the next day with a smile and an envelope containing rent money. You were too weak to come out of our room.

This time, seeing me alone, she took me aside and asked, "What is your sister suffering from? Where is she today?"

"She's at the hospital."

"Good. It was time. I'm here to help you, so don't make my job difficult! What do you need?"

This time, I wanted to yell. To beg her to understand. To have her look through the apartment. To take us away by force. But she lost her resolve.

"Are you unable to speak or something? And your sister. You let her get sick and didn't lift a finger? What world do you come from!"

This woman couldn't understand. And I was afraid of Amira. She would never forgive me if I betrayed her.

All of our parents' pride rests within you. I merely bent to your will.

The social worker didn't come back again. The building manager slipped a letter under our door stating that city hall had taken care of our unpaid rent.

They believed they'd done what was necessary. From that point on, they would have nothing to reproach themselves for.

I try to take you to the window—to force you to get up. "Look, you just need to take a couple of steps to change everything. For destiny to deal its cards again."

You motion for me to go away. I come closer. Your eyes are getting wider. I lift up your shoulders. Your head flops backward. You're crying, and I leave you alone.

Paris shelters us and ignores us. Nearby is the elegant Georges Brassens Park, where ladies stroll, carrying bags stuffed with chocolate for children's snacks. A little farther off is the opulence of the Porte de Versailles's exhibitions.

I can see the Vanves flea market from here. Every weekend, young women my age with their blonde hair pulled back and jackets or furs hanging down over their sneakers look, feel, ask, and then leave with their dream find in the trunk of a car.

In the afternoon in that same place, the dreams change shape as do their vendors. The shopkeepers come from where we do.

While the connoisseurs pass by one another, other stands go up. Valuable clocks, cups with thin gold designs, pedestal tables, and hat boxes make room for blue-and-white striped vinyl bags from Barbès, ready-to-wear clothes in pure synthetic fibers at fifty francs apiece, plastic tablecloths, fabric covered in sequins that come off at the slightest touch, cassette tapes, alarm clocks, and fake Swiss watches. Once the Gauls' France leaves, our people believe themselves to be in conquered territory. The souks of Marrakech and Algiers come to life. Housekeepers from the Maghreb wander around with their hair covered or colored and with double-basket carts and temptations filling their eyes. Our coreligionists fill their baskets, chat between purchases, and leave happy, as if they'd gotten access to their most ardent desires. They must be right. Apart from these stands with low-quality goods, what meaning does their life have in this country?

Here at home, we don't even have the bare minimum now. Not one superfluous object—nothing saved up for hard times. Amira, do you remember when I disguised our emigrant life in front of our stunned cousins? Before your eyes, which were filled with bitterness. Do you know what I should have told them if I hadn't forced myself to lie—if I had allowed myself to lift the veil?

Listen to what I would have said: "Dear cousins and friends of Alouane, don't be fooled. Entrance into the Franks' kingdom is illusory. We have a perfect grasp of their language, Amira and I. However, this hasn't even given us the privilege of breaking through its administrative barriers or claiming success of any sort. Even Pierrot—who mangles the language, who twists it up worse than Mama does, who sullies it with his alcohol-laden breath—is convinced he speaks it better than we do. Because he thinks it belongs to him—just like everything else . . . But how can Pierrot be made to see reason? Like my mother, he has his own sense of logic. He wouldn't be alive without it.

"Come closer, dear nieces, daughters-in-law, and beloved aunts! Come here so I can open the doors upon the place I've described as heaven. Look at the reality we find ourselves in and compare it to the tales I cradled you with. Look around us. Admire this building filled with its tiny windows, eternally broken elevator, and stairwell that smells like piss. Look at this city's filth that coats the walls as well as our souls. It's made of chemical dust and layers of overlapping selfishness—a pile of toxic clouds and its equivalent in cowardice. Listen to the infernal noise from the beltway that's so close it has become a miserable lullaby for our nights and a sonorous background for our nightmares. Tour the cramped rooms with their low ceilings, dissymmetrical tiling, cracked windows, and excrement-colored paint.

I'll open our closets for you—look at the emptiness hanging from the two plastic coat hangers that serve as its armature. Count the cockroaches that wander around on a desperate search for a crumb to place under their antennae. They're our competition. They still have the strength to migrate elsewhere in search of survival. Not us. Not our loyal cat. You see it sleeping on the unplugged fridge that long ago forgot what it was supposed to be used for. Check in all of the drawers—there isn't a single can of food, a grain of rice, salt, or wheat. What's left? Just a few final traces of crushed sugar granules beneath the sheepskin. Here is the country where we live, where we grew up, and that we prefer to Algeria.

"Come closer! I'm not selling you illusions. I'm selling you real misery. I'm selling you France!"

After the social worker came by, nobody tried to disturb our solitude. Or tried to find some other way to convince us not to die. We'd concluded that we were right.

I remembered what Pierrot had said. And the doctor and social worker's severity. I thought no one would understand how I could bear to watch you slip away before my eyes without doing anything to help you. To watch death insidiously slide into your body, paralyze your limbs one by one, plane away your flesh and your resistance, shape you into a hollow ball of pain and a perfect haven of misery. But here I am, watching death's work, allowing suffering to run its course.

They don't doubt that this is your wish and mine. They don't know how far despair has taken us, the determination it has etched into our wills, or the tragic spell it will soon use to seal off our youth.

I know what's pushing you to die, and I'm dying from it with you. Because I'm the oldest, I must watch over your passing and follow you soon after. Delay my death in order to be there for your last breath of life. I must die from your pain before dying from mine.

Did I have any other solution? Can we linger over our own

wounds when those we love reveal deeper ones? Can we tell our own life story when other people's is the only thing holding it together? Did I even have a life? Deprived of words and choices, stuck between all of you, watching you disappear one after the other?

This morning, you spoke to me. You know you're but a few hours away. You asked me not to call for help—not to try to save you.

I thought about our mother. She passed away a year ago, and with the same determination. Yes, I'm certain she created an illness and then applied herself to making sure she would die of it. In silence. Without having learned how to betray pain with words. Like us, she was a victim of this inability to say what hurts, of this modesty that forbids our hearts from pouring outward.

Asking for help often tempted me to the point of obsession. Hunger tore apart my stomach, made me dizzy, prevented me from thinking clearly. I would have done anything for a mouthful of bread, a handful of rice. I knew you suffered more than I did without your saying anything at all. But the image of old people digging through the trash cans at the markets came to me. I thought of Djamila's shame.

Today, panic-stricken by your warning, I found the strength to go to the landing. I heard Rose turn her key. I hid. I waited for her to leave. I went down one floor, and I found myself in front of the building manager. He came toward me.

"You're ill!" he grimaced.

I shook my head. I struggled to stay upright. To hide the shaking in my legs.

"How is your sister?"

"Very well," I whispered.

Perhaps he was waiting for me to confide in him. Does he think people share their sadness as easily as they can their joy? That they open the door to their pain with hospitality?

He's mistaken. This is no one's business but yours and mine.

I came back up without looking at him. I worried that you were already dead. I heard his footsteps quickly racing down the stairs.

I found you in the same position, eyes closed, very weak breath. As though you had turned your head toward the other side of the light. As though my voice no longer reached you.

The building manager came up a little later that evening. He knocked on our door for a long time, but he didn't hear a single noise.

Tonight is Christmas. I opened the windows. The city lights cover up our misery. Everyone believes that everyone is happy. And everyone is simply delighted to believe this.

Paris is growing quiet—can you hear? I imagine that the mob of little kids has deserted the "vindows," as Mama would say. The wood-and-wax marionettes continue their pantomime, beat out a rhythm, turn in circles without getting out of breath; they sometimes fall off the track late at night when there is no one there to see them.

Children caress the marble on their fireplaces. Dreaming out loud. I think Rose is all alone. Writing postcards to her anonymous correspondents. Mr. Zana is probably where he chose to feel at home. I miss Geneviève. The clinking of silverware comes up from Pierrot's. The smell of roast turkey. Pierrot caresses his belly. He snuggles into his armchair, and he belches a waft of acidic wine and foie gras. I no longer hear your wheezing.

Little sister, do you hear what I'm telling you? You look like you're asleep. Listen one more time. I've come to the end. Then you'll know your parents' story. The story you didn't want to know. And they did nothing to teach it to you. I should have gathered up their greedy memories on my own in order to give them a past—to reconstitute their existence, trip after trip, at random through words and allusions. What interest is there in talking about oneself when you were raised with respect for the clan? A few stolen words about their youth, their struggles, the reasons for their exile. They hated the personal narrative and had no fondness for confession.

How could they have thought that we would understand them with just this—that we would do exactly as they had?

I've often asked myself this. Listen, little sister, to what I saw in my father's eyes on those afternoons he spent in his wheelchair gazing out the window at Paris's roofs.

"Once upon a time, in the village of Alouane . . . We had the illusion that we were happy."

Night has fallen.

Your limbs are frozen, and your breathing has slowed. I hear a confusing noise. The building manager must have alerted the local police. They're no doubt coming with medical help. In white uniforms.

But don't worry, little sister—they won't rip my plan to die with you away from my heart. My plan to escape from them.

Of course, they'll be shocked by our *state,* as Béchir's wife would say. Scandalized that we gently let our existence float off to break upon the two shores' blue waves.

But you and I know the truth. The truth that the police will search for in vain. We know we will die from this country. From its indifference, from its cruelty, from the impossibility of integration. We will die from Algeria, too. From its distance, from its cruelty, just like we will from the impossible hope of returning there. From this life our parents built upon an illusion: "a mirage of happiness named France."

Little sister, you're dying of this France, just as my mother died of her Algeria.

And I'm dying of my inability to invent another country.

In vain, I search for your gaze. Should I try in spite of everything to save you—to call for help before it's too late? I'd have to find the strength to do it. And I put all the strength I had into these final words.

I can't hear you breathing anymore, little sister. Yet there isn't the slightest noise out there. I must have been wrong. Those aren't the police. It must be the cat. I'm shocked that he didn't leave us. I can't bring myself to kick him out. Rose might take care of him.

You're not moving anymore. You look like the emaciated children from Sudan they show on television. You're like a doll that's been taken apart. Like a dwarf tree.

Don't you think, Amira? You look like a dwarf tree. You aren't smiling? You've got nothing to say? Answer me, Amira! You're still alive, right? Answer me! It's not true that you're gone? Not yet. I'm not done talking to you yet. Words are powerless . . .

Say I didn't kill you! I really did hope. I don't want to see you asleep forever. I'm waiting for a miracle.

They came. They ripped you from my arms; I wasn't able to protest. They knelt over your body—they lifted it, light as an armful of dead leaves. They put it on a stretcher and got ready to go down the stairs.

I tried to get up on my own. I demanded to go with you. They didn't listen to me. A young woman stuck a needle in my arm.

To die of hunger in a rich country. How tasteless in the eyes of the majority. Rose will blame us for shunning those who reached out. Pierrot, for tarnishing France's honor. Adel, for tarnishing Algeria's. Those in good health, for having spit on life.

Who will say a prayer over Amira's grave, this grave dug through misery?

GLOSSARY

Al-Jazair: Algeria in Arabic

baccalauréat: France's high school exit exam

baroud d'honneur: originally, cannon powder fired off to indicate victory

bled: term that signifies an immigrant's town of origin; in French, the term is pejorative

chèche: a cotton scarf used as a headwrap

Casbah: citadel in a North African city; older portion of a city

darbouka: a goblet-shaped drum

djellaba: long robe, piece of clothing with a hood

djinn: invisible being able to influence humans

douar: a group of dwellings most often bringing together families claiming to be the descendants of a common ancestor; village

Eid: Muslim holiday and festival

Eid Esseghir: Muslim holiday and feast marking the end of Ramadan

fellaga: Algerian combatant fighting for independence from France (1954–62)

fellah: farmer

FLN: Algeria's National Liberation Front

gandoura: traditional North African robe for men or women, usually made of silk or cotton, with an embroidered V-neck

gouirra: term signifying foreign Christians, non-Muslims, Western Christians; synonym for *roumi*

hammam: Moorish bath

haram: term meaning both "forbidden" and "sacred"

harem: term for a man's female entourage and for the women's living space

harki: a term referring to Algerians who supported the French during the war of independence (1954–62); after the war, they were viewed as traitors; tens of thousands were killed and nearly one hundred thousand fled to France

harkou: henna design

houri: term for the virgins who reside in Muslim heaven and are companions to the faithful

khôl: cosmetic used to darken the area around the eyes; antimony powder

kilim: woven rug

maquis: underground forces

marabout: an important holy person of popular veneration; holy person's tomb; shrine honoring this person

mashrabiya: ornamental ventilation screen covering window spaces in Islamic architecture; screens provide privacy and allow people inside to see but not be seen

Night of Ordainment: the night when the Koran was first revealed to the Prophet Mohammed

pied-noir: Algerian-born French person during the colonial period

Ramadan: religious fasting during the month of Ramadan (ninth month of the Muslim calendar)

Restos du Coeur: a charitable organization providing food to those in need; started by the French comedian Coluche in 1985

roumi: (originally "Roman") designation for a French (i.e., Christian) man or a foreign man; other form is *roumia* (feminine)

sadaqa: charity

safsari: white silk or linen veil

Sonacotra: acronym for the "Société nationale de construction de logement pour les travailleurs" (National Corporation for the Construction of Workers' Housing). The company, renamed Adoma in 2007, built and managed dormitory- or hostel-like living quarters for immigrant workers suitcase carriers: the middlemen who helped transport funds out of France to support the FLN during the Algerian War

souk: North African marketplace

surah: chapter of the Koran

wadi: a streambed that becomes an oasis following heavy rains

zarda: a large meal, feast

AFTERWORD

Susan Ireland

The French-language writer Fawzia Zouari, who was born and grew up in Tunisia but has lived in France since 1979, has established herself as a prominent author of both fictional and nonfictional works. Partly because of her own experiences, the topic of migration lies at the heart of her oeuvre and is reflected in many of the themes that recur throughout her novels—cultural hybridity, betrayal, the wounds of exile, and the quest for freedom, for example. An ardent champion of women's rights, Zouari examines in particular the different types of boundaries crossed by women who seek to define their own identities. The trajectories of her female protagonists illustrate the diverse ways in which women negotiate displacement, whether chosen or imposed, and their journeys thus provide an answer to a question raised by Zouari in one of her early essays: "How can one come to understand an Arab woman's experience of exile?" (*Pour en finir* 41).[1]

Of France's former colonies in the Maghreb, it is Algeria, rather than Tunisia or Morocco, which has produced the most French-language writers. While the first of their texts formed part of the struggle against colonization, which culminated in the war of independence (1954–62), many of their later works have spoken out against the status of women in postcolonial Algeria and have drawn attention to problems faced by the independent nation, including the decade-long combat against militant Islamists who sought to destabilize the government. In addition, authors of Algerian descent living in France, often the children of laborers recruited to work in France after World War II, have highlighted issues related to immigrants' lives in the metropole, and their work now constitutes a substantial, much-studied corpus. In contrast, the number of French-language writers from Tunisia, which was a French protectorate until 1956, is comparatively small, and women remain a minority, whether they write in French or in Arabic. The first French-language novels by Tunisian women were not published until 1975, and of the forty works of fiction in French which received the Golden Comar Prize (Tunisia's most prestigious literary award) between 1997 and 2009, only fourteen were written by female authors (Kréfa 112). Since the Jasmine Revolution (December 2010–January 2011), however, more Tunisian women have started to make their voices heard, whether as bloggers, essayists, or novelists, and in 2016 the top prize for an Arabic-language novel was awarded jointly to two women, Emna Rmili and Nabiha Aïssa, while Zouari was the corecipient of the award for a work in French (*Le corps de ma mère*). The author of eleven books since 1989, Zouari has addressed the concerns of several generations of women and has treated a variety of subjects ranging from the situation of Algerian immigrants in France to the unfolding of the revolution in Tunisia. For this reason, she has earned the reputation of being a committed writer who does not shy away from potentially contentious cultural and political issues.

Education and Formative Experiences

Zouari was born in 1955 in the village of Dahmani in the region of Kef in northwest Tunisia.[2] Here, she received a traditional upbringing, speaking Arabic as her first language and learning the Qur'an at the age of five (Zouari, *Je ne suis pas* 15). After obtaining her high school diploma (baccalauréat) in 1974, she studied French literature in Tunis, where she met her future husband, and went on to earn a doctorate in French and comparative literature at the Sorbonne. Subsequently, she worked for the Institut du Monde Arabe in Paris from 1987 to 1996 and has written for the weekly newsmagazine *Jeune Afrique* since 1997.

Zouari often associates her reactions to her conservative upbringing with the notions of transgression and betrayal. Indeed, she has described an Arab woman's decision to leave her homeland as a subversive act, pointing out that she herself has crossed geographic, cultural, and linguistic borders by moving to France, marrying a Frenchman, and choosing to write in French rather than Arabic (*Pour en finir* 42). In *Le corps de ma mère,* her latest and most openly autobiographical work, which recounts her quest to uncover her dying mother's life story, Zouari sheds light on some of the main reasons for her own rebellion against traditional gender roles. Although the narrative focuses on the mother's experiences as a woman in a patriarchal society, it also portrays her as an authoritarian figure and as the enforcer and embodiment of many of the rules that her daughter would later reject. In addition, Zouari emphasizes that her mother fiercely respected the taboo against revealing intimate details about the family and personal relationships; for this reason, Zouari's gravest sin in her eyes—besides marrying a Frenchman—was to have become a writer (*Le corps* 49). Zouari is thus well aware that, for her mother, the publication of *Le corps de ma mère,* which reveals family secrets and is, furthermore, written in French, would have constituted another form of transgression (*Le corps* 12, 232).

When speaking of her mother in the 2015 essay *Je ne suis pas Diam's,* Zouari depicts one dramatic event in particular as a turning point in her life, relating that in June 1960, her mother announced her decision to take her three eldest daughters (aged nine to thirteen) out of school and symbolically burned their schoolbooks and writing materials, thereby making them prisoners of the home and depriving them of their freedom (18–20; *Le corps* 58). As she looks back on this moment, Zouari credits it with being the origin of her promise to herself that she would complete her studies and never wear a headscarf (*Je ne suis pas* 20). However, when her turn came to have her books burned, her father, influenced by Tunisian president Habib Bourguiba's emphasis on educating girls as well as boys, intervened and insisted that she stay in school. Many years later, Zouari continues to express her gratitude to him for standing up to her mother and for placing learning above tradition (*Je ne suis pas* 86), thus setting her off along the path that would lead to her becoming a writer.

Nonfictional Works and Women's Rights

The literary critic Josefina Bueno Alonso has remarked that although relatively few North African and sub-Saharan women have historically chosen the essay as a genre in comparison with their male counterparts, a more substantial body of nonfictional writing by women has emerged since the 1980s (61, 66). Zouari, who is cited by Alonso, is the author of five book-length essays that deal primarily with the wearing of the veil, women's writing, and feminism in the Mediterranean region. In her first essay, *Pour en finir avec Shahrazad* (1996), Zouari examines a broad range of issues related to writing and to representations of Arab women. In particular, she rejects the role of victim and demands the right to determine her own identity, indicating that she does not recognize herself in the many stereotypical images of oppressed Arab women that regularly appear in the Western media (24–26). At the same time, the numerous references to Scheherazade in this essay and in Zouari's work in general draw attention to another archetypal figure, the legendary storyteller of the *Thousand and One Nights,* who is often portrayed as a model for Arab women writers. Zouari finds this model oppressive, however, because Scheherazade only recounts the stories of others and does not speak for herself. In contrast, Zouari claims the role of creator and extols the pleasures of self-expression, arguing that writing, for her, is part of a process of self-discovery rather than a means of survival (12, 136).

Zouari's concern for women's emancipation extends well beyond the domain of writing. In her 2012 essay *Pour un féminisme méditerranéen,* she calls on women across the region to promote intercultural dialogue at a time when nationalism and fundamentalism of various kinds are on the rise. In this work and in other articles and essays, she expresses her pride in the fact that Tunisia has been a leader in the area of women's rights in the Maghreb and the Middle East, and she highlights the pioneering role played by figures such as Tahar Haddad, who in the 1930s argued that it was necessary to emancipate women if Tunisia was to become a modern state (*Pour un féminisme* 39).

Zouari also draws attention to the importance of the Personal Status Code enacted by President Bourguiba in 1956 and later strengthened by his successor, Ben Ali. The code introduced major reforms that benefited women, especially as regards marriage, divorce, child custody, and employment. As Zouari observes, it abolished polygamy and the practice of repudiation, made schooling for girls obligatory, legalized abortion, introduced family planning, and mandated equal pay, even for agricultural workers (*Je ne suis pas* 23). In addition, single mothers now have the right to give their own family name to their children, and rape, sexual harassment, and domestic violence are recognized as punishable offenses (Lichter 340). On the occasion of the fiftieth anniversary of the Personal Status Code, Zouari highlighted the significance of these reforms, affirming that "the true Tunisian revolution . . . was to have instituted an incomparable personal status code, in women's favor, half a century ahead of its time!" (Middle East Media Research Institute). She went on to express her strong belief that, despite the rising tide of Islamism, Tunisian women will not be willing to give up the body of laws that protects them and will not allow history to be reversed. In her words: "Men, my dear friends, it is too late. Tunisian women, who are accustomed to freedom, will not go back to the house. They, who have learned to hitch their own destiny to the future of their country, will not let themselves be intimidated by the sirens of puritanism, even if it triumphs elsewhere in the lands of Islam" (Middle East Media Research Institute).

Zouari is also the author of three essays on the veil. The first of these, *Le voile islamique,* provides a historical study of the different meanings attributed to the veil in Muslim societies and in the West; the second, *Ce voile qui déchire la France,* focuses on issues related to the so-called headscarf affair in France, the debates surrounding the controversial proposal to introduce legislation banning the wearing of the headscarf in public schools. Finally, in *Je ne suis pas Diam's,* Zouari responds with dismay to Diam's's decision to wear the *hijab* and abandon her successful career as a rapper. Zouari addresses her comments directly to Mélanie Georgiades (Diam's) and forcefully conveys her inability to understand how an educated person who has converted to Islam could voluntarily resolve to wear the veil, which Zouari views as a symbol of subjection (21). Zouari concludes the essay with a passionate call for young Muslim women in France to follow a different path and to advance the cause of Islam by using their talents in fields such as science and artistic creation (158). In order to underscore her vision of what constitutes a positive role model for young women, Zouari asks rhetorically which Diam's serves Islam better: the dynamic, engaging singer, whose performances reflect her creativity, or a Diam's who has returned to the home and whose voice is now heard only in praise of the veil (158).

The Early Fictional Works

Zouari's novels are often inspired by historical figures or by events reported in the news. *La caravane des chimères* (1989), for example, a fictional biography based on research Zouari conducted for her doctoral dissertation, recounts the life of Valentine de Saint-Point, the great-niece of the celebrated Romantic poet Alphonse de Lamartine. Saint-Point, whose trajectory is reminiscent of that of the more famous Isabelle Eberhardt, traveled from France to Egypt, converted to Islam and adopted the name Rawhiyya Noureddine, supported the cause of Arab nationalism, and eventually died in Cairo in 1953. In *Pour en finir avec Shahrazad,* Zouari notes that very few women are mentioned in histories of travel writing, arguing that they deserve more attention because their evocations of the Other are generally more nuanced, more realistic, and less eroticized that those of their male peers (32, 36–38). Zouari's account of Saint-Point's voyage helps remedy this situation, and her protagonist is the first of many women in her work who cross borders in search of freedom and self-expression. The rich narrative, which focuses on Saint-Point's spiritual journey, also evinces the nationalist and feminist agendas that Lora Lunt sees as characteristic of historical novels by contemporary Tunisian women writers (135). Indeed, Zouari highlights Saint-Point's opposition to French and British colonial rule in the Middle

East and portrays a range of strong female characters who question prescribed roles for women in both France and the Middle East.

Ce pays dont je meurs (1999), Zouari's second fictional work, is her best-known novel and has been the subject of many scholarly analyses.[3] Like *La caravane des chimères,* it was inspired by real events, in this case a report in the press in 1998 that a young woman of Algerian origin living in Paris had allowed herself to starve to death and that her seriously undernourished sister had almost died. Zouari's imaginative re-creation of the story, which is described on the front cover of the paperback edition as a "drama of integration," recounts the increasing disillusionment and broken dreams of two generations of an immigrant family from Algeria. Like many contemporary authors, Zouari places the ethnic body at the center of her work in order to examine what Jennifer Terry and Jacqueline Urla have called "embodied deviance"—the ways in which certain body types are figured as deviant in relation to the norm (13). In *Ce pays dont je meurs,* the effects of immigration on the protagonists entail changes in bodily awareness in both generations of the family, and Zouari employs recurrent corporeal images to convey the nature of the relationship between France and its Others. In particular, she makes a strong indictment of the French model of integration, which promises "acceptance to those marked as culturally or racially Other, yet indefinitely postpones the fulfilment of that promise" (Kemp, *Voices* 73).

The use of corporeal images in the depiction of the father serves to portray the progressive erasure of his identity. In *Masculine Migrations,* Daniel Coleman posits that narratives of migration constitute "an ideal site in which to explore gender in moments when it is unstable and in crisis" (xii). *Ce pays dont je meurs,* which accords a prominent role to the father (Ahmed), gives expression to this type of instability. An older immigrant who has lived in France for twenty-five years, Ahmed represents the many Maghrebi men who came to France as skilled or semiskilled workers between the 1940s and 1970s and exemplifies the period of family reunification and permanent settlement. Recruited primarily in rural areas, the Maghrebi workers came for the most part from traditional patriarchal cultures in which "economic power, moral authority, and social responsibility" were invested in the father (Ben Jelloun 59). Selected for their good health, but often illiterate and speaking little or no French, they have generally been viewed as a silent generation that was largely invisible in French society. As several prominent psychiatrists and sociologists have noted, however, these men frequently gave voice to their sense of powerlessness through a form of body language in which a constellation of ailments spoke eloquently of their difficulty coping with the trauma of exile. Tahar Ben Jelloun, for example, observes in his study of the psychosomatic illnesses of male immigrant workers that the frequent references to impotence in the patients' testimonies are often explicitly related to migration—"My penis is homesick" (159)—and suggest a change in self-image that expresses itself physically and psychologically as loss of manhood. For Ben Jelloun, the appearance of this "impotent Maghrebi expatriate" (182) is the result of the exploitation of immigrant workers in a capitalist system, and he repeatedly highlights the desire to harness the workers' strength while concomitantly denying their existence as men and as sexual beings (12).

Early in *Ce pays dont je meurs,* the depiction of Ahmed as a "manly" young immigrant is juxtaposed with references to anonymity in the workplace, the loss of individuality underscored by the fact that the French boss calls all his immigrant employees by the same generic name (Momo) (42). Subsequently, images evoking the diminution of the body reflect the first stages of loss of manhood—"Ahmed had shrunk a bit. He didn't have the same imposing presence as before. He sat with his chest bent over his plate, as if he were nearsighted. . . . His gestures lacked assurance" (42). At this point in the narrative, however, Ahmed still maintains his patriarchal role within the home in an attempt to bridge the gap between the gender models he grew up with and the place he is assigned in French society. The narrator remarks, for example, that, "at home, he made an increasing number of remarks and allusions that attested to his male power" (42). In similar fashion, his adoption of a stereotypical item of French clothing, the beret he wears to work and takes off as soon as he comes home, represents his negotiation of two sets of cultural codes and his efforts to blend into French society. At the same time, references to sexual potency, symbolized by the creaking of the marital bed, suggest the possibility of his being able to retain a sense of dignity and belonging when he is not at work. Indeed, his expression of his sexuality is associated with nostalgia for Algeria and with the stability represented by traditional gender roles, and making love to his wife is explicitly described as "his way of regaining possession of his country. The country he would never forgive himself for leaving" (28). As Anna Kemp contends, Ahmed at times seems to be performing the role of patriarch in an exaggerated manner "as a reaction to his sense of emasculation on French soil" (*Voices* 80) and in an attempt to remain "master of his destiny" in the space of the home at least (Zouari, *Ce pays* 28).

The fragile equilibrium between Ahmed's two worlds is broken when a work-related accident (a back injury) puts him in hospital for eight months and leaves him permanently disabled, thus making him a good example of what Madelaine Hron calls the "maiming of the father"—the recurrence of accidents, injuries, and illness in depictions of male Maghrebi immigrants in literary works (93). After the accident, references to his lifeless muscles, his unsteady gaze, and his wheelchair highlight the loss of his role as breadwinner, which constituted the core of his identity in France. Likewise, with its evocation of the figure of the eunuch, the description of the reconfigured family as "a strange kind of harem, without a man" (30) underscores the idea that the father has moved definitively from the workplace to the home, a space traditionally coded as feminine. At this point, his inability to work is accompanied by his abdication of his paternal authority—"Unproductive, he persuaded himself that his authority, just like the lower half of his body, no longer had any effect" (30)—and the earlier allusions to sexual prowess are replaced by references to impotence that signal the disintegration of his identity. For the narrator, the cessation of her parents' lovemaking marks the last stage of her father's dispossession and confirms Ben Jelloun's contention that, for someone raised with Ahmed's worldview, "there is no place or role for a man who is sexually 'mutilated'" (64).

As in the case of Ahmed, changes in the mother's appearance and body image reflect her alienation and sense of diminishment. Djamila comes from a respected family and is proud of her ancestry, but she experiences a loss of status in France, where she finds herself relegated to a lower position in the social hierarchy, that of "banal immigrant" (43). The weight she puts on soon after she arrives in France constitutes a symptom of her homesickness and serves as a form of compensation for the losses associated with exile. Even her pregnancy, a different type of weight gain, is portrayed as a means of forgetting the misery of her life in France, and her daughter Amira's birth is linked to memories of her native land. When she has to accept work as a cleaner after Ahmed dies, other bodily ailments such as her migraines and her sore hands suggest the suffering of a woman who "always expressed herself through her body rather than words" (87). Changes in her appearance also suggest a psychological split that reflects her increasing inability to reconcile her two worlds. Her reluctant efforts to adapt to French norms of dress and behavior, symbolized by her removing her veil and wearing her daughter's sneakers to work, lead to her feeling foreign, and the use of expressions such as "disguise" and "creating a double for herself" (11) underscore the idea that, while she may outwardly appear less culturally Other in the eyes of dominant French society, she has become a stranger to herself. The problems she experiences with badly fitting clothes reinforce the impression that her body and sense of self no longer coincide, and, in the same way that Ahmed removes his beret when he comes home, Djamila changes into her Algerian clothes and symbolically spends time cleansing her amber-colored skin, one of the primary markers of her difference, as if it had somehow been soiled by her venturing out into French society.[4]

In contrast, the transformation she undergoes during family vacations in Algeria suggests wholeness and a renewed confidence in her body, which is valued and desired by others: "she became a complete person again. A few steps in the airport in Algiers were enough for her to rediscover, through the desire in men's eyes, that she was still a woman" (87). However, as Kemp remarks, each member of the family "seems engaged in a series of role plays that emphasize their urgent desire to belong, while simultaneously underscoring the impossibility of realizing this desire" (*Voices* 80). This role-playing extends to Djamila's return to her village where, in order to maintain her pride, she feels she must project an image of successful integration and insists that her daughters participate in the masquerade by pretending to be happy and well-off. Ironically, this fictitious story created for the family's relatives restores for a brief period the dignity and social status that Ahmed and Djamila have lost in France, a situation that the narrator understands very well: "My father didn't say anything about this marketing operation. His pride and virility also depended upon it" (45).

The trajectory of the two daughters, Nacéra and Amira, again highlights the ways in which the body serves as "a sorting mechanism whereby the culturally dominant and the culturally marginalized are assigned their 'proper' places in the body politic" (Smith 10). Both daughters want to believe in the promise of integration but are acutely aware that their body type consigns them to a marginal place in society. Nacéra, for example, refers to her curly black hair and her dark-brown skin when evoking her deviance from the norm, asserting: "I felt so different in terms of my language, my looks, and my thoughts that I only had one challenge . . . to be like everyone else" (49). This consciousness of her difference is reinforced by her frequently moving between the worlds of home and school: although the teachers do their best to transform the sisters into "children of the Republic" (52), Nacéra notes that "the mold shattered at the threshold of our apartment. . . . It fell apart when it came into contact with the blood-red henna that coated Mama's hands" (52).

The portrayal of Amira's anorexia, which begins when she is twelve, at first represents her attempts to erase the Algerian side of her identity. Indeed, her refusal to eat is linked to the wish to be "a hundred percent French" (54), a desire reinforced by her adoption of a French name (Marie) and her portrayal of herself as being of Italian origin. Ironically described as a French illness by her Algerian parents who do not understand its cause, her anorexia is also linked to images of excess and removal. In particular, her view of her Algerian identity as a form of excess that she must "get rid of" (80) if she is to fit into French society diametrically opposes her to her mother, whose weight gain symbolizes her desire to cling to an Algerian identity associated with the appreciation of "curves" (57). However, her anorexia soon comes to signify an impossible metamorphosis—"No, she could not have a different body, nor could she change her destiny" (81)—and serves as a powerful expression of the feelings of dispossession created by her encounter with the sorting machine. Unable to modify the place assigned to them by the dominant cultural group, the sisters are forced to abandon "the illusion [they] entertained that [they] could be taken for people from here. That [they] could be looked upon lovingly by the Republic" (60).

If Amira's anorexia begins as an expression of her efforts to be seen as fully French, it later stands for her agency in the face of a situation she deems unacceptable. As Kemp puts it, Amira's "destroying her body seems to be the only way of claiming ownership of it" (*Voices* 88). At this juncture, as the sisters increasingly withdraw from society, rarely leaving their apartment, Amira's self-starvation conveys her radical rejection of the place that she and her sister have been assigned, that of "second-class citizens" (Zouari, *Ce pays* 106). Her anorexia can thus be construed as a rebellion against the impasse in which she finds herself—marginalized in France and not belonging in Algeria either—an impasse faced by many young people of immigrant descent. In Nacéra's words, "everything made her sick. Her parents' past and her own future" (85). Paradoxically, then, Amira's resolve to die of starvation can be read as "a heroic act of free will" (Hron 124), a "perverse victory" (Kemp, *Voices* 88), and the fact that her anorexia is "resignified as a rejection of the country that has rejected her" (Kemp, "Le passeport" 57) manifests her refusal to compromise by accepting a place in the margins.

Ultimately, the two generations of the family are united through a form of body language that reflects the wounds of exile and immigration. The image of the inanimate body, which links mother and daughter at the end of their lives, represents their shattered dreams, recalls the father's immobility after his injury, and prefigures their death. Nacéra remarks that "the same murdered hope lived in their motionless bodies" (Zouari, *Ce pays* 96), and the mother's death, like her daughter's, is explicitly associated with her exilic state and is depicted as a kind of suicide: "Her love of Algeria, relegated to the depths of her being, had poisoned her body" (103); "I'm certain she created an illness and then applied herself to making sure she would die of it" (117). Likewise, the fact that the daughters are described as "ghosts" (109) highlights their invisibility in society and suggests their desire to remove themselves from it. In this sense, the title of the novel, which portrays France as a fatal disease, evokes both the suffering caused by exile and the despair associated with the difficulty of integration. As Nacéra puts it when speaking to Amira at the end of her life: "Little sister, you're dying of this France, just as my mother died of her Algeria. And I'm dying of my inability to invent another country" (121).

By recounting her family story, Nacéra reveals the functioning of the sorting mechanism from the perspective of those who are subjected to it. Her ironic comparison of herself to Scheherazade, the archetypal storyteller, focuses attention on the reasons why she has chosen to tell her story: whereas Scheherazade is traditionally associated with survival and the saving of women's lives, Nacéra tells her tale not in order to ward off death but to "kill time while waiting for the end" (63). Most importantly, by explicitly linking France with "indifference," "cruelty," and "the impossibility of integration" (121), she raises the crucial question of how many more of those marked as Other will be excluded from full participation in society before the situation changes.

In the last part of the novel in particular, the narrator underscores the physical effects of extreme hunger which turn Amira into "a hollow ball of pain" (115).[5] Because of the prominent role given to bodily and psychological suffering, the text has been read as a classic example of "the politics of pain" (Hron 33), that is, as a work that sensationally exposes an individual's or a community's wounds in order to gain sympathy and demand reparation. At several points, however, as Kemp has cogently argued, *Ce pays dont je meurs* seems instead to engage in a critique of the politics of pain and its implications for the culturally marginalized.[6] While the novel does unquestionably evoke the deep wounds caused by exclusion and humiliation, Amira and her family refuse to assume the position of supplicant in order to obtain recognition on "the competitive empathy market" (Kemp, "Le passeport" 59), where it is necessary to "make people feel sympathy in order to exist" in their eyes (Zouari, *Ce pays* 95). Nacéra is also well aware that her family's trajectory is not spectacular enough to give it value on this market. Indeed, the use of the adjective "banal," which recurs at several key moments in the novel—the transformation of the mother into "a banal immigrant" (43), "a father lost to a banal accident" (94)—suggests that the family's story is not exceptional but represents a kind of norm. This emphasis on the ordinariness of the family's situation makes Zouari's condemnation of France's relationship with its Others all the more forceful in that it highlights society's indifference to the systemic discrimination created by the sorting machine.

La retournée and *La deuxième épouse*

Zouari returns to the topics of border crossing and identity in her two most recent novels, both of which take up the interrelated themes of migration and betrayal in order to contest traditional views of what constitutes appropriate behavior for women.[7] Taken together, the two works create a multifaceted portrait of the ways in which Maghrebi women are choosing to transgress cultural norms and are confronting issues such as patriarchal authority and polygamy. In *La retournée,* a Tunisian woman (Rym Ben Amor) who had defied her family and left her homeland in order to marry a Frenchman goes back to her native village (Ebba) for the first time in fifteen years when her mother dies, and is treated by the villagers as a "retournée"—a term that connotes "treachery" and "repudiation" (120).[8] Rym describes herself as a rebel, and her decision to move "outside the law of the clan" (*Pour en finir* 41) makes her a symbol of disorder and a threat to the status quo. Indeed, the villagers see themselves as the wounded party, and the terms employed to characterize Rym's conduct—"scandal" (57), "unforgivable offense" (55)—underscore her transgression. Rym's young daughter Lila serves as an embodiment of her mother's offense, her blue eyes and her French native tongue symbolizing "the unheard of" (208), her mother's marriage to a foreigner. Rym's behavior signifies dishonor for her family, and her depiction of herself from their perspective reinforces the notion of a legacy of shame and of the betrayal of family and community: "I'm the Ben Amor child who went astray. The one who makes the men in the family hang their heads" (55). Rather than evoking the motif of the prodigal son who is welcomed back into the fold, Rym's homecoming thus suggests an unhealable rift and stresses the fact that the conservative community of Ebba views her behavior as an undesirable model for future generations of women.

The gradual revelation of the factors that motivated Rym's decision to leave Ebba emphasizes that, while the villagers associate her departure with betrayal, Rym sees it as liberating. Casting herself in the role of betrayed rather than betrayer—"this country betrayed me" (28)—she highlights the lack of opportunities afforded women in 1980s Tunisia, and her description of Ebba and its inhabitants evokes a timeless world in which nothing has changed since she left. The group of men who come to meet her when she arrives in the village, for example, are associated with imprisonment and represent the patriarchal society she fled fifteen years earlier. The portrayal of the roots of Rym's rebellion also focuses on the role mothers play in perpetuating societal attitudes toward female children. In this context, Rym's mother symbolizes tradition: under pressure from her in-laws to have a son, she viewed her daughter as a "sinister gift" (24), and Rym emphasizes the negative impact these male-centered views have on the formation of a girl's identity. Her mother's refusal to allow her to go on to university after obtaining her high school diploma was the immediate catalyst for her elopement,[9] and Rym points out, for example, that her mother transmitted unhealthy ideas about women's sexuality, especially the importance attached to virginity as a symbol of family honor.

The depiction of Rym's return to Ebba and her evocation of childhood memories also serve to create a satirical portrait of the encounter between tradition and modernity. The many descriptions of the village women's lives provide a wealth of information on traditional attitudes toward such issues as gender relations, sterility, and superstitious practices. Now a journalist and painter living in Paris, Rym represents a more emancipated position and is often surprised by the recriminations of the local women, most of whom align themselves with the men, accuse her of immorality and impiety, and condemn her for going out alone. At the same time, the emphasis on the villagers' unchanging lives foregrounds Rym's continuing infraction of prescribed roles for women. When she goes to the cemetery where her mother is being interred, for example, her presence there breaks with received religious practices, which do not allow women to attend burials. At this point, the juxtaposition of her uncle's indignant reminder, "Tradition forbids it" (26), and Rym's acerbic response—"I unlearned submission a long time ago" (26)—creates a parallel between the tradition/modernity dichotomy and the themes of subjection and freedom.

In addition, Rym's romance with her childhood friend Moncef reinforces her role as a figure of disruption. Like Rym, Moncef has left Ebba, is highly educated, and works in an urban environment (Tunis). However, when Rym begins a relationship with him, she comes up against two types of taboo. One the one hand, she is criticized for not respecting the rules of propriety, as she openly goes on walks with him and invites him into her house; on the other hand, the fact that he is the son of the Ben Amor family's former maid makes his relationship with Rym unacceptable because of the difference in social class. In contrast, she is ready to see him as a long-term partner only if "he is capable of violating taboos" (242).

Finally, Zouari uses Rym's transgressions to address the question of women and the law. The actual dispute portrayed in the novel, Toufik's attempt to disinherit Rym's sister Noura and her aunt Zina, links him with the theme of betrayal and emphasizes the theme of women's rights. On another level, the patriarchal order itself is symbolically put on trial as Rym comes up against entrenched attitudes as soon as she sets out to protect Zina and Noura. Indeed, the recurrent references to gender in the episodes related to the inheritance dispute serve to emphasize that law is viewed as an exclusively male preserve. In order to defend Noura and Zina, Rym appears before two kinds of court and, in each case, finds herself on trial for taking on a role traditionally reserved for men. First, in the unofficial family hearing, which takes place on her uncle's patio, Rym is judged and found guilty for assuming the role of advocate. Here, her confrontation with the men in her family is again framed in terms of submission and authority, as is evident in the fact that the uncles and male cousins assembled on the patio have been summoned there to witness "how the elders know how to deal with women who disobey" (135). Secondly, when Rym goes to the local court to begin formal proceedings against Toufik, her subversion of gender roles is underscored by references to her unexpected familiarity with legal terms, and the satirical descriptions of her interactions with the court clerk and with the local authorities who try to intimidate her forcefully bring out Zouari's belief that women should fight for their rights. By having Rym win her lawsuit against Toufik, Zouari not only provides a concrete example of a woman's ability to obtain justice for her family but also leaves the reader with no doubt as to who the guilty party is in the broader sense—in the case against the patriarchal order. Rym's legacy is thus one of empowerment, and her role as a model for other village women is highlighted in episodes in which some of them come to her for advice about legal questions and treat her as an authority figure.

Whereas *La retournée* takes place in Tunisia, *La deuxième épouse* is set in France and was inspired by the assassination of an Algerian Member of Parliament in Paris in 2003 and the subsequent revelation that he was living three different lives. In Zouari's imaginary version of the events that led to the murder, a series of women recount their stories after a lawyer is killed by his mother-in-law for hiding the existence of his first wife. In this polyphonic narrative, the main characters represent diverse forms of migration and include a first-generation Algerian immigrant (Halima), the daughter of a *harki* (Rosa),[10] a Tunisian novelist whose husband is French (Farida), and a young woman of Algerian origin (Lila) who has grown up in a suburban *cité* (housing project). Like *La retournée, La deuxième épouse* focuses on gender relations, and Zouari again links the female protagonists to the themes of betrayal and injustice. In particular, the murdered husband (Sadek) symbolizes infidelity, his betrayal underscored by his being given the posthumous title of "perfect polygamist" (206). Over the course of the novel, Sadek is described by the three women who shared his life, becomes the subject of Farida's new book, and is commented on by many of her friends. The composite portrait of him that emerges from these interwoven voices places his unfaithfulness at the center of the text and enables Zouari to put the practice of polygamy on trial.[11]

For the second wife, Rosa, who is a magistrate, marriage to Sadek represents acceptance and a homecoming of sorts after her family's traumatic uprooting from Algeria. As she puts it, "He became our Algeria" (30). At the beginning of the novel, however, Rosa lies in a coma in a hospital bed and addresses her thoughts to God after trying to commit suicide because she has discovered that her husband has another wife and family in Toulouse. Here, her dramatic self-description underscores from the outset the emotional impact of Sadek's betrayal—"I, Rosa Bennaceur, who died of my own free will, after loving, after suffering the outrage of polygamy" (43)—and she expresses her conviction that God, "the great magistrate in the sky" (43), will rule in her favor in the case against her husband.

In contrast, Sadek's first wife (Halima) and his young "fiancée" (Lila) use him as a means of achieving independence. Halima, who married Sadek when she was seventeen, learned from her mother that "It's in their [men's] nature to be unfaithful" (104), and her father and grandfathers, like Sadek's, practiced polygamy. When marrying Sadek, then, Halima had no illusions about his remaining faithful and saw him above all as way of escaping the rural environment in which she grew up. Like Rym in *La retournée,* Halima wished to move beyond the limitations that circumscribed her life, and she does not hide the fact that the prospect of moving away from her village constituted an integral part of Sadek's appeal: "He wasn't really a Prince Charming . . . I couldn't have felt any desire for him without the idea of a voyage" (89). Ironically, it is Sadek's secret polygamous relationship with Rosa that gives Halima the time and the freedom to become independent, and his frequent absences are associated with her bodily and psychological transformation. While Sadek is in Paris with Rosa, Halima goes out alone, gets to know French women in her neighborhood, improves her French, takes evening classes, adopts the name Emma, and learns to appreciate her body and make her own decisions. This strong desire to "change her skin" (100) reflects her rejection of traditional gender roles and constitutes the final stage of her migration.

Lila Salem, Sadek's intended third wife, is a younger version of Halima and shares with her the strong desire to break with the environment in which she grew up. While Halima sought to leave an Algerian village, Lila hopes to find a way out of a *cité* in Creil, a municipality to the north of Paris. The border Lila wishes to cross, the dividing line between the so-called "immigrant" *banlieues* (suburbs) and mainstream French society, is thus primarily sociocultural in nature, and when Farida first sees Lila, she immediately identifies her origins and her desire for social mobility. At the same time, Farida's evocation of the "misogyny found in the *banlieues*" (221) introduces the theme of gender relations in the context of families of Maghrebi origin. Her negative comments are echoed in Lila's references to the perpetuation of traditional patterns of patriarchal authority and to the existence of a polarized view of women predicated on the purity/prostitute dichotomy. In contrast, Lila presents herself as a modern young woman who wishes to express her sexuality without being perceived as a "whore" (196), and she sees Sadek as the best of her options.

Sadek's polygamous relationship with his wives and his fiancée also serves to link the theme of betrayal to that of injustice. Although he is ostensibly the victim of a crime in the whodunit sense, it is Sadek who is tried and found guilty by the women in the novel, just as the patriarchal order is judged in *La retournée.* As in *La retournée,* too, Zouari depicts two different types of trial in *La deuxième épouse,* the fictional trial that takes place in the book Farida is writing and the official court hearing in which Rosa's mother is tried for murder. Farida views her new book as contributing to the struggle for women's rights: she places Sadek's unofficial trial at the center of her text, and the excerpts she reads to Rosa in the hope of bringing her out of her coma all involve this event. The venue chosen for the trial, a patio somewhere between France and Algeria, where Emma, Rosa, Lila, and Rosa's mother are gathered around Sadek's body, is depicted as an intimate women's space and thus contrasts with the episode in *La retournée* in which Rym is judged by the men in her family on her uncle's patio. In *La deuxième épouse,* Farida's summary of the situation portrayed in her book—"Three women, three generations, three lives caught in the snare of infidelity. . . . And a dead braggart. A monster" (243)—clearly designates the polygamous Sadek rather than Rosa's mother as the perpetrator of a crime. Indeed, the conversation that takes place between the women on the patio underscores their shared condemnation of Sadek's duplicity, as they move from insults and recriminations to curiosity and complicity, gradually working out how Sadek managed to hide his infidelity and revealing increasingly personal details about their lives with him.

In the final pages of *La deuxième épouse,* the trial that takes place in a French court reinforces the idea that Sadek is the guilty party. Here, Rosa eloquently defends her mother, who is associated with honor and dignity and is given tragic stature through a comparison with Antigone.[12] At the hearing, Rosa's testimony also returns to the seriousness of Sadek's conduct when she affirms that his betrayal, rather than her father's *harki* past, caused her deepest wound (312). The portrayal of the two trials, along with the judgments made by Farida's friends, thus invites the reader, too, to condemn Sadek's "crime" and to espouse Rachel's view that, "No woman can remain unmoved in the face of such a betrayal" (106).

Throughout the novel, Farida's observations on the book she is writing and her frequent allusions to Scheherazade establish a strong metafictional dimension which highlights the creative process and asks what it means to be an Arab woman writer today. Several of Farida's friends compare her to Scheherazade when she takes on the role of storyteller in the hope that her words will save Rosa. Like Zouari, however, Farida vehemently rejects Scheherazade as an emblem of Arab women writers, explicitly stating "I don't want to be Scheherazade" (123), and objecting that this model is outmoded and conveys the message that her mission is to "entertain the male sex" (123). By making a distinction between the roles of storyteller and creator, Farida echoes the views of Zouari herself, who proposes to replace Scheherazade with the Sumerian goddess of writing Nidaba, who, for her, represents the freedom to create "purely for pleasure" (*Pour en finir* 136). For Farida, then, as for Zouari, the act of writing opens up a space of freedom and resistance, a world men cannot control and is, for this reason, equated with the abolition of borders.

At the end of both *La retournée* and *La deuxième épouse*, the protagonists contemplate moving on, and Zouari thus brings the reader back to the theme of migration. Distressed by her own husband's infidelity, Farida wonders whether she should leave France, while Rym envisages going to Canada with her new partner, Moncef. These strong female characters, who both seek justice for women, do not hesitate to challenge traditional cultural norms and, as such, illustrate Zouari's belief that, although they may be painful, subversive journeys ultimately lead to greater opportunities for women to carve out their own path. As she puts it, "Every border an Arab woman crosses is a taboo that falls, a resistance that gives way, a cry of pain, but of the pain of a mother-to-be, which heralds a new birth" (*Pour en finir* 46). Just as migration is synonymous with creation for Zouari herself, as it brings with it the freedom to write, so, too, the exiled woman is an ultimately positive figure in her work since she represents the possibility of bringing about change and symbolizes the emergence of "an Arab identity which is engaged in the modern era. . . . An Arabness that is on the march and is being transformed" (*Pour en finir* 49).

Notes

1. All translations are my own, except those from *I Die by This Country*. For a general discussion of the motif of exile in Zouari's work, see Amel Fenniche-Fakhfakh's *Fawzia Zouari: L'écriture de l'exil.*

2. Zouari indicates in an interview with Philippe Douroux for an article in *Libération* that there is some doubt about the year of her birth, with her mother maintaining that she was born in 1956 and her father, in his capacity as local *cheikh*, recording it as 1955 (3).

4. For a discussion of this point, see Hollis 221.

5. The narrator also describes the effects of hunger on herself: "Hunger tore apart my stomach, made me dizzy, prevented me from thinking clearly. I would have done anything for a mouthful of bread, a handful of rice" (117).

6. See Kemp's "Le passeport de la douleur ou rien" for an insightful analysis of Zouari's critique of the politics of pain.

7. Zouari is also the author of *J'ai épousé un Français,* which was written under the pseudonym Aïcha Kessler. Inspired by Zouari's own experiences, this text recounts in humorous fashion the life of a Franco-Moroccan couple (the husband is Alsatian and the wife Moroccan).

8. See Anne Marie Miraglia's "Le regard double de *La retournée*" for an analysis of the theme of return in *La retournée.*

9. The episode of the burning of the sisters' schoolbooks recurs in *La retournée* and is witnessed by Rym (46–48).

10. The term *harki* refers to the Algerians who supported the French during the war of independence (1954–62); viewed as traitors by many of their compatriots, thousands of them were massacred or were forced to flee to France at the end of the conflict.

11. Polygamy is illegal in Tunisia. In Algeria, a man may marry up to four wives, but the number of polygamous marriages is very low.

12. Rosa finally comes out of her coma when Farida asks her who will plead her mother's cause. She explains her mother's actions in cultural terms and relates them to migration.

BIBLIOGRAPHY

Alonso, Josefina Bueno. "L'essai africain au féminin: Parcours thématique." *International Journal of Francophone Studies* 9.1 (2006): 61–77.

Ben Jelloun, Tahar. *La plus haute des solitudes*. Paris: Seuil, 1977.

Coleman, Patrick. *Masculine Migrations: Reading the Postcolonial Male in 'New Canadian' Narratives*. Toronto: University of Toronto Press, 1998.

Douroux, Philippe. "Fawzia Zouari, dévoilée." *Libération*. Dec. 28, 2015. Web. Sept. 20, 2016.

Fenniche-Fakhfakh, Amel. *Fawzia Zouari: L'écriture de l'exil*. Paris: L'Harmattan, 2010.

Hollis, Isabel. "Metamorphoses in Migration: Fawzia Zouari's *Ce pays dont je meurs*." *Expressions of the Body*. Ed. Charlotte Baker. New York: Peter Lang, 2009. 213–30.

Hron, Madelaine. *Translating Pain: Immigrant Suffering in Literature and Culture*. Toronto: University of Toronto Press, 2009.

Ireland, Susan. "Deviant Bodies: Corporeal Otherness in Contemporary Women's Writing." *Nottingham French Studies* 45.3 (2006): 39–51.

———. "Masculinity and Migration: Representations of First-Generation Maghrebi Immigrants Living in France." *Masculinities in Twentieth- and Twenty-First-Century French and Francophone Literature*. Ed. Edith Biegler Vandervoort. Newcastle: Cambridge Scholars Publishing, 2011. 76–92.

Kemp, Anna. "'Le passeport de la douleur ou rien': Fawzia Zouari's *Ce pays dont je meurs* and the Politics of Pain." *Contemporary French Civilization* 41.1 (2016): 49–67.

———. *Voices and Veils: Feminism and Islam in French Women's Writing and Activism*. London: Legenda, 2010.

Kessler, Aïcha. *J'ai épousé un Français*. Paris: Plon, 2010.

Kréfa, Abir. "Corps et sexualité chez les romancières tunisiennes." *Travail, genre et sociétés* 26 (2011–12): 105–28.

Lichter, Ida. *Muslim Women Reformers*. New York: Prometheus, 2009.

Lunt, Lora. "Reclaiming the Past: Historical Novels by Contemporary Women Writers." *Institut des Belles Lettres Arabes* 62.2 (1999): 135–58.

Middle East Media Research Institute. "Tunisian Feminist Fawzia Zouari on 50th Anniversary of Tunis's Personal Status Code: 'In Tunisia, Women

Have Become Just Like Any Other Man.'" Special Dispatch 1314. Oct. 11, 2006. Web. Aug. 14, 2016.

Miraglia, Anne Marie. "Le regard double de *La retournée:* Entre hier et aujourd'hui, entre Ebba et Paris." *Les espaces intimes féminins dans la littérature maghrébine d'expression française.* Ed. Robert Elbaz and Françoise Saquer-Sabin. Paris: L'Harmattan, 2014. 293–313.

Terry, Jennifer, and Jacqueline Urla, eds. *Deviant Bodies.* Bloomington: University of Indiana Press, 1995.

Smith, Sidonie. *Subjectivity, Identity, and the Body: Women's Autobiographical Practice in the Twentieth Century.* Bloomington: Indiana University Press, 1993.

Zouari, Fawzia. *La caravane des chimères.* Paris: Olivier Orban, 1990.

———. *Ce pays dont je meurs.* Paris: Ramsay, 1999.

———. *Ce voile qui déchire la France.* Paris: Ramsay, 2004.

———. *Le corps de ma mère.* Paris: Joëlle Losfeld, 2016.

———. *La deuxième épouse.* Paris: Ramsay, 2006.

———. *Je ne suis pas Diam's.* Paris: Stock, 2015.

———. *Pour en finir avec Shahrazad.* Paris: Cérès, 1996.

———. *Pour un féminisme méditerranéen.* Paris: L'Harmattan, 2012.

———. *La retournée.* Paris: Ramsay, 2002.

———. *Le voile islamique: Histoire et actualité, du Coran à l'affaire du foulard.* Paris: Favre, 2002.

Recent Books in the Series CARAF Books

Caribbean and African Literature
Translated from French

Yanick Lahens
Aunt Résia and the Spirits and Other Stories
Translated by Betty Wilson

Mariama Barry
The Little Peul
Translated by Carrol F. Coates

Mohammed Dib
At the Café and The Talisman
Translated by C. Dickson

Mouloud Feraoun
Land and Blood
Translated by Patricia Geesey

Suzanne Dracius
Climb to the Sky
Translated by Jamie Davis

Véronique Tadjo
Far from My Father
Translated by Amy Baram Reid

Angèle Rawiri
The Fury and Cries of Women
Translated by Sara Hanaburgh

Louis-Philippe Dalembert
The Other Side of the Sea
Translated by Robert H. McCormick Jr.

Leïla Sebbar
Arabic as a Secret Song
Translated by Skyler Artes

Évelyne Trouillot
Memory at Bay
Translated by Paul Curtis Daw

Daniel Picouly
The Leopard Boy
Translated by Jeanne Garane

Fawzia Zouari
I Die by This Country
Translated by Skyler Artes